Outcast

....

Valerie Himenez

Contents

Under the Blue Blood Moon

"Hurry Bill! It's coming out!!" Claire's shrill cry echoed in the corridor. Her husband Bill was in a panic grabbing her bag in the second floor of the house. There were thuds from the objects falling from his every move. Bill, the pack's Beta known for his bravery and strength has turned clumsy and was sweating cold sweat all over his body. The panic, the excitement and nervousness has risen to his head he can't hardly breathe. Claire was finally giving birth to their first born!

"Bill!!!! My moon goddess! What's taking you so long?!?" Claire shouted at the top of her lungs. A mix of agitation and pain in her voice. She held her belly tighter. The little baby's kicks were unbearable. "I'm here, Honey. We're leaving.. Let's go.." he emerged from the stair's landing almost falling, face panic-stricken and held her wife with trembling hands. "For goodness sake Bill, hold yourself together! It's me who's going to give birth but it's you who looks like shit!" Claire's face was very pale now and wrinkled trying to overpower the pain. She gripped in her husband's arm a little too tight.

"Congratulations Mr. & Mrs. Mayfield, it's a she! A very healthy baby girl! " beamed Dr. Luke Ross, the pack doctor. His graying hair shining like a halo in the light of the flourescent lamp above. The couple were overwhelmed with unexplainable joy. For the first time after trying for almost 3 years, the moon goddess had given them the child they have been praying for. Tears of joy were streaming down the couple's face. Overjoyed and satisfied especially Claire. She extended her arms to receive her baby. "She's beautiful. Very beautiful... " she uttered amidst her tears. Her husband leaned closer to her and kissed her forehead. "What shall we call her?" Bill asked. "Mona Elara. She's blessed by the moon goddess herself and the blue blood moon above us." Claire said softly kissing her baby's head, still asleep in her chest. "Mona Elara Mayfield. As beautiful as you are... " Bill said lovingly to his wife. Claire looked at his husband and gave her a kiss and the couple shared that beautiful moment until a knock on the door interrupted them.

A tall and muscular man came striding from the door. He was handsome with his slick bronze brown hair combed neatly backwards. He has a chiseled jawline and enigmatic hazel eyes. His crooked nose did not downturn his looks either, it just added power to it. His very presence is magnetic and powerful. That is because he is the alpha of the pack. William Jones is the alpha of the Black Moon Pack.

"Alpha..." the couple bowed their heads at the sight of their alpha. "How are you Claire?" he asked in his powerful tone. "I'm feeling better now, Alpha. Thank you for the visit." Claire said while her husband reached for the alpha's hand and they did their secret handshake. "May I?" Alpha William inquired hesitantly, asking permission to see her baby. Claire just nods her head and smiled.

"What a beauty!" the Alpha exclaimed. "She got your looks indeed! I wonder what Bill has contributed? " he said jokingly to Bill. "Maybe my skills and strength you'll see Alpha... " Bill said proudly. "Of course she will be. Another worthy and strong wolf in our pack!" Alpha William valiantly proclaimed and both of the men laughed.

"She's cursed." A voice from behind the Alpha spoke. Nobody in the group noticed her coming. All eyes looked at the source of the voice. It was the Luna speaking. She's in her late thirties, elegant, graceful and stoic. Her chestnut brown hair is in a fancy bun and she was wearing a blue dress. As blue as the moon above.

Luna Miranda Jones was another power in the pack. Born from the Alpha of a neighboring pack the Scarlet Moon pack, another strong and respectable clan in the North, she exudes the aura of a royal. But in contrast to her husband, Alpha William Jones, she is colder and stoic than her mate.

"The baby is cursed." She repeated coldly. Her lips tightly pursed. "What exactly do you mean?" exclaimed the Alpha. His eyebrows furrowed deeply making lines in his rather perfect skinned face.

"Look at her eyes." she answered without blinking. And so, all of them looked down at the baby, now wide awake and smiling to all the faces above her. And for the first time, they saw her eyes. One is blue and the other is amber. First were curious looks, followed by shock and then by fear. For a moment nothing moved, even their breath were still. Until, the baby's shrill cry broke the stillness of the night.

The Promise

"**D**addy..." eight year Mona Elara Mayfield knocked hesitantly at her father's study. She doesn't want to disturb her father but she must. She wants him to sign a waiver for the school camp to the Northern woods that will be on Friday until Sunday. She placed her head on the door to hear what's going on. It has become her habit actually. But this time, she shouldn't have. She heard her fathers laughter and another high-pitched giggles. It has gone quiet for awhile. Mona knows that she shouldn't disturb him now, for sure she'll receive a beating if she did. Apparently, her father is having a good time with another slut.

But even if he signed the waiver or not, his father doesn't care on whatever she will do anyway. Her father cannot stand her presence and she don't know why. But she actually has an idea, based on what she hears from the murmurs of their neighbors and what the other kids are calling and teasing her. Their accusing looks that makes her cower in a corner. Her father has not said a word about her mother's death but she knew, he is blaming her for it.

On the other side of the door, Bill was having a good time with her new girl Brenda. She's just 27 and an experienced whore. His new girl Brenda is definitely a bombshell. Sexy, alluring, young. But he just can't push it through for a face she wont dare forget keeps forming in the back of his mind, smiling back at him. Brenda was pressing kisses onto him and he pushed her away, he saw defiance painted across her pretty face.

"Shit!" Bill cussed under his lungs. "Bill, honey, What's wrong?" Brenda asked. "Come on..." she coaxed him and reached for his arm but he yanked it off. "Get out!" he forcefully said. "What the heck Bill?!?" she protested "Get your ass out of here!!! " he exploded. Brenda whimpered, fixed her clothes and reached for the door. "I don't want to see you again!" he said with finality. Brenda looked back as she glared at him. "Just so you know Bill? You are an asshole!" she spat at him and closed the door with a thud.

Bill paced back and forth in the room, his hand unconciously combing his hair. He grabbed the bottle of vodka and gulped it down.

"I'm sorry Claire. I'm so sorry.... " he said while looking at her portrait on the wall. Claire was beyond beautiful. She had long dark brown curls. Her green eyes were full of life and mirth, her lips were red and Bill knew that he misses her more than ever.

"I miss you, my darling. So, so, so much. " he pressed his hand towards his eyes to stop the tears that were trying to escape. A knock on the door brought him back to his senses.

"Daddy, can I come in? " said the little voice. It opened slightly and Mona sticks her head in. She looks apprehensive at him.

"What do you want?" he said coldly. "I-I just want you to sign this..." she held a paper to him, her hand trembling. He grabbed the paper and read it. "Camp? Three days?" he said. She tensed up. Looking more afraid. He opened a drawer and rummaged for a pen and signed it without second thoughts. He pushed the paper to her and looked at her intently. The little girl can't hold his gaze. "Th-thank you, Daddy... " she stammered and took the waiver. She was about to leave when he said sternly. "And Mona, don't cause any trouble again. You know what will happen if you do."She nods her little head and left as swiftly as she can. He can't stand her presence. It brings back the pain that he shut out in the deepest parts of his heart. Whenever she's there, he can't stop himself from hating Mona. He still remembers that day. Very clearly.

A week after Claire gave birth to their daughter, she got very sick. An uncurable and unknown sickness struck her. Giving her chills every night and a fever that never goes below 38. She tried to hold on for as long as she could but it weakened her defenses. But even if she was terribly ill, she would want to hold her daughter. She would spend hours and hours looking at her and crying because she cant stay with her for so long.

"Just kill the child." Luna Miranda whispered to him. "That's the only way Claire will be saved." The Luna came in for a visit and sheaid this to him one day. They were in the far corner of Mona's room, Claire is sitting beside the baby crib.

But Claire overheard their conversation. She suddenly looked mad and furious.

"Over my dead body! No one will touch my child!!! " Claire screamed at them. Both of them looked at her and fury covers her face. " Why do you want to kill my child? And Bill, don't tell me you will consent with her absurd plan!" Claire said angrily, now shaking.

"She's cursed Claire. She'll cause your death and misfortunes will befall to the pack! We must take her!!!" Luna Miranda said at her even fiercer. Reminding Claire who she's talking to. She is the Luna and her decisions equates to that of the Alpha. If it emdangers the pack, then she has to take action.

"No!!!!" Claire shouted and then she shifted. Her wolf Alena came in and attacked Miranda. The Luna on the other hand was caught off guard, she stumbled back. Bill immediately grabbed his wife with all his force. But she just tossed him aside. Miranda shifted as well and they struggled with one another. It was havoc. The baby cried like crazy while the two women fought with each other. The door swung open and the Alpha came in. Obviously was not happy to see the commotion.

"STOP THIS NONSENSE INSTANTLY!!!" The Alpha's voice thunders in the room. Both women stops from attacking each other and went to the sides. Alena, Claire's wolf went to the baby to protect her.

"You are not going to touch my baby! None of you!" she threatened

"Calm down Claire. We are not going to take her nor kill her." the Alpha voiced. Claire is not dumbed. She knows the moment she lowers her guard, they'll take her precious baby."I will curse all of you and ten of your generations if anyone will touch my baby!!!" she continued angrily.

"No one will take her! Calm down Claire." it was Bill, coaxing his wife. Claire just looks at them angrily. Hating them for trying to take her child. For accusing her of curses they never knew if real.

"Claire, I swear. No one will harm your child. She is one of the daughters of the pack. She is worthy of protection. Don't worry. " William said calmly, winning Claire's trust. He walks slowly towards the baby's crib, measuring his every step. He knows that one wrong move can make things or break otherwise. Claire is wary, growling, threatening. He reaches the crib and touches the baby's hand. Claire growles louder but the Alpha remains calm and recited the words that changed Claire's defiance into trust.

"I, William Jones, Alpha of the Black Moon Pack, swear in front of you Claire Mayfield to protect Mona Elara Mayfield, your daughter, for the rest of my life and my sons after me. No one will harm her under my watch. No one will try to kill her. No one will touch her! She will be safe as long as my bloodline is alive." said Alpha William with all his will. Now, an Alpha's words cannot be broken. He was already bonded to Mona the moment he spoke his promise. He then exhales."Now, Claire, calm down." he said kindly. In a tone not that of an Alpha but that of a friend

Only after hearing the Alpha's words, Claire calms down and transforms back to her body. She fell in her husband's arms wearily. Bill covers her naked body with a blanket. Miranda just glared at her. She stood up with all her strength and walked towards the Alpha. She reaches for his hand and cupped them with both of her hands.

"I, Claire Mayfield, accepts this promise. This is an unbreakable vow and even death will not undo it." She took her husband's hand and placed it on top of their hands.

"You, William Jones, Alpha of the Black Moon pack and his son and son's sons after him, together with my husband, Bill Mayfield, solemnly swear to protect my daughter Mona Elara Mayfield with all their life and the next." she chanted. A silvery thread started to move from the tips of her fingers and moved gingerly to William and Bill's hand, tying them together in a knot. "Breaking the vow will mean death to both of you and your bloodline. This is our unbreakable vow." she finished.

"Stop this madness!" Miranda shouted. William's other hand stopped her on her steps.

"This is our unbreakable vow." Both men finished the chant. Claire smiles peacefully. The kind of smile you give when you are both happy and content. Claire is leaning on her husband, looking down at their child, now peacefully asleep. Bill knew she won't stay long as he feels her weight grew heavier. She looks up at the alpha and whispers her thanks, then she closed her eyes for sleep.

Later that day, Claire died while holding her precious baby in her arms.

The Camp

The unbreakable vow between Claire, William and Bill eight years ago seemed to have no effect today. The only power it has was keeping Mona in the Black Moon Pack alive yet miserable.

Mona's life was miserable eversince her mother died. Her father cannot stand her presence, she'll receive a beating just for breathing. The adults are all hesitant to even look at her, and the children, exclude her in their games. She's not part of any circle. She have no social life. And it's okay. As long as she have her Granny Josephine. She is the only person who took her in. Cared for her even if she was treated badly by others, loved her even if her own father cannot. Believed in her even if she doubted herself.

Josephine has been the housekeeper of the Mayfield home eversince Bill himself was just a kid. She took care of him herself and now his daughter. She served the Mayfields all her life and Bill respected her like his own mother. At 70, she is still as strong and sharp as she was seventeen. "Granny, look! Daddy signed it!" Mona said brightly at her, the paper in her hand. "That's great, Honey. I know you'll have a great time there." she hugged the girl. For her age, she is rather small and skinny. She has light blond hair, almost silver with streaks of brown strands. She hate the thought of sending her away to the camp but her father cannot care less. The other pups treat her badly and it hurts her to see wounds after her ventures outside. Mona on the other hand just ignores all of it. She loves the outdoors. She has fascination with plants and flowers and painting. No wonder, it has become her hobbies. "This is not the life that you deserve, sweetheart. You should be happy playing outdoors with friends... " her mind speaks sadly. "I can't wait to see the majestic falls! Just so you wait Gran, I'll draw a splendid picture of it for you!!!" Mona said even brighter looking up at her with eyes twinkling with delight.

It was her eyes that has become the object of ridicule. Her mismatched eyes were a curse and may bring bad luck to anyone who sees it and eventually, the pack where she belongs. But for Josephine, it was the eyes of the goddess herself. She sees purity and warmth in her eyes. The right eye was blue, it was pale blue like the blue moon when she was born. And the left was a beautiful amber. The goddess' eye as she called it. "I'll start packing!" Mona swiftly run upstairs to her room. She's one ball of energy indeed. She just shakes her head and started to prepare dinner.

" I told you before William, but you did not believe me!" Miranda was yelling in front of the Alpha. "5 of our finest men died of this rouge attacks! I told you! One misfortune followed by another. This happens because of that cursed girl! Because you were stupid not to believe in me!!!""Stop it Miranda...My head's already aching..." he said keeping his cool while massaging his temples. Last night, the guards watching over the territory were attacked by rogues. Last winter, a severe snowstorm struck them. 2 families died in an avalanche near their home. Last autumn, kids were sick. Even his son Tristan got sick. During the past eight years, a lot of unfortunate events has happened in the pack. Although, it is foolish to blame an innocent child for it all, he is now starting to believe his wife. However, her constant nags irritates him even more. And at top of that, there was the unbreakable vow. It means death for him and his bloodline once he reversed the vow. His head ached even more."This has to stop! We have to kick her out of the pack!" Miranda said firmly. He looked at her furiously. "Don"t touch the girl!""I won't... I have a plan. " she said with a smirk.

"You take care of yourself Sweetie." Granny Jo was sending Mona off to the camp. "Yes Gran! I promise I will. " she said sweetly. "Your lunch is in your bag. And in case you get hungry along the way, there are more snacks in the pockets." Granny Jo said with a wink. The school buses were waiting in the Pack's Square a few meters away from their house. "I'll have to go! See you soon Gran!" she kissed the old woman's face. She looked up and saw her father peeking behind the curtains, she waved her hand to him and send him a kiss. He immediately closed it off. "See you, Sweetie. Have a good time!" Josephine said while waving her hand. Mona sprinted to the square.

When Mona reached the square, the other pups were already there. She immediately went to the last of the line. Her place. "What is she doing here?" one girl whispered rather loudly to her friend while eyeing her. In the crowd of children, she definitely stands out. The Black Moon pack is known for having dark colored hair - from brown to black. Only she has a lighter toned hair. No other kid has hair as light as hers, not even light brown. She unconciously touched her braided hair. She has perfect-ly straight light blonde almost silver hair with streaks of brown strands. Mismatched eyes, one pale blue, the other amber. Creamy skin under her khaki camp uniform and lips as red as apples. But no one appreciates her looks. Not once. Not ever. That is because she is the cursed child. She instantly lowers her eyes. At eight, she knows how to avoid trouble, only that trouble loves her anyway.

"Move aside, freak!" a chubby boy named Burris Long shoved her almost pushing her. "It's okay Mona. You cant see them. You cant hear them." she said to herself. Slowly, the children went in the bus. As usual, no one wants to sit with her nor offer a seat to her. She looked around until she reached the back of the bus, but a group of boys has occupied it already. Looking angrily at her, she knows what they mean. She have no choice but to stand up all through an hour of bumpy ride to the northern woods. The bus went to a sharp turn and she wasnt able to hold still she fell face first on the floor. Everyone laughed. She repeated her mantra in her head. "Ignore them Mona. You cant see them, you cant hear them."At last, after an ardous drive they finally reached the camp. Fun activities as well as delicious foods awaits!

The camp master came up. A petite yet athletic woman with a pixie cut hair. The kids fall in line. "Listen up Campers!" her yell echoed around. For a small woman like her, she has a ground-breaking voice. "I am your Camp Master for this year's camp feast!" She announced. "My name is Tori Kane. And all of you should follow all my orders once you are in my camp! You have to follow your troup leaders, they will orient you with the do's and don'ts while you are here." A group of 12 year-olds came marching in. There were 10 of them. They are the troup leaders. "Mess hall's on the right. Quarters are on the left. Camp haven lies behind me and endless excitement lies therein!" She said energetically.

"Now, all of you will be grouped into ten teams, each with 10 members each. 5 boys and girls. Selected by alphabetical order, " Mona tensed up when she heared the order. It only means she will be grouped with the meanest bullies in town. Oh no. "When your name is called, come forward and receive your group's badge and stay behind the troup leader assigned to your group. Understood?!?"An echoing yes responded. Ms. Kane started calling out names. There were ten groups in all. All named after flowers. Rose, Tulips, Dandelion, Iris, Hibiscus, Orchid, Daisy, Bluebell, Lily and Snapdragon. She's in Lily. Ms. Kane's voice continued calling out their names.

Logan, Myrtle

Lundres, Rhoda Jane

Madison, Faye Paula

Mason, Julia

Mayfield, Mona Elara

The moment her name was called, everything seemed to stay still, even the wind. All eyes filled with indifference looked at her. She stepped up and received her badge. A Lily flower was engraved in the bronze badge."Let me pin it." Ms. Kane said kindly. "Thank you, Ma'am." She did not dare to look in her eyes.

She moved towards a 12 year old boy with chestnut brown hair and a piercing stare in his hazel eyes. She recognized him immediately. He was the alpha's son, Tristan Jones, as enigmatic as his father and was their assigned troup leader. All her groupmates were looking at her with disgust especially Paula and Myrtle.

"Yikes, she's in our group! Now, this means she'll jinx our chances of winning the games!!" Paula eyed Mona with hatred. Myrtle just glared at her. She lowered her eyes while passing by them until she reached the end of the line and waited until everyone was settled in a group.

"Now, let this year's Camp Feast begin!!!" Ms. Kane boomed in her energetic megavoice, all birds flew away.

Into the Night

Each team were assigned a cabin to stay for the entire camping trip. Theirs was a quaint little log house. The interiors were warm and cozy, Mona just wanna sit near the fire and open her books. But it just impossible. Her groupmates immediately occupied the room and are already playing tag. She's not excited with her team at all for she happens to belong to a group of meanies. Myrtle and Paula proves to be bad girls, paired with Bruno Horn and Burris Long already bullying the other pups. Now she's sure that she will be in trouble.

"Oi! Who do we got here?" Burris' mocking voice echoed in the room. "It's little Miss Silver rat, eh?" he approached her and brusquely dragged her in the center of the room. She dropped her bag in the process. That's what they call her, a rat because she's nothing but a toy for the other pups. Easy to pick on whenever any of them got bored. To them wolves, rats are not even edible, they are disgusting and dirty it causes disease. And that's her for them.

"Look here! Look at that cursed hair!!! Still trying hard to belong in this pack with those dirty brown strands??" Paula laughed heartily and pulled Mona's hair back so that Mona can see each of their sneering faces. "Say something, freak! Say something!!" pulling it even harder. A tear is forming at the corner of her eye."Oh, no, little Miss Silver rat is starting to cry... What a crybaby!!!" Myrtle teased , the others followed suit chanting crybaby. "Don't you have anything to say little rat??" Paula sneered.

"Well, I say you stop or I'll send you home at this instant." Tristan Jones said as he came walking in. His authoritative voice is enough to froze Paula in her spot. She jerked her hand off Mona's hair. The latter's braid was now a mess. The other pups moved back as if cornered.

"Rule number 1. No one is to hurt or harm anyone during this camp. This camp aims to promote camaraderie and friendship and what do you think are you doing?" Tristan continued pacing back and forth the common room. The culprits just bowed their heads lower, no one dares to return the piercing gaze of the next alpha in line. He continued reciting all the rules they have to adhere."Girls' room is on the left, the boys' at the right. Settle your things in your quarters and be back after a minute. Lunch is ready in the mess hall." As he said it, he stopped in front of Mona's bag. He stooped and picked it, then he slowly paced towards Mona, still seated like a lump of rag on the floor. Mona grabbed her bag without looking at Tristan. He's just doing his duty as the Troop Leader. She must not assume more than that. All the pups hurriedly picked their bags and went to their respective quarters. After a minute, they are back and are falling in line. They started walking out towards the Mess Hall while she stood rooted on the spot. "Why are you not moving, Mayfield?" Tristan inquired. "Have you not heard? To the Mess Hall now..." he ordered. "Sorry Troup Leader, but I want to go to the comfort room. My stomach is unwell..." she lied. She just wanted to be alone. "We can have you checked by the Camp's Nurse if your stomach hurts." he replied, a hint of worry in his voice. "No, thank you. Granny packed me medicine if something like this happens." For the first time, she looked at him, directly in his eyes. He looked away instantly. Really, no one can stand her even Tristan. "Okay but meet us at 4 o'clock in the Camp's Square for the first task." he finally said then walked out.

At last, she have some peace. She went into the Girl's room . Inside were two double decker beds with white and green checkered covers and a small cot beside the window. All of their bags were on the beds. Of course, she'll take the cot. She placed her bag there. She carefully took her lunch box and placed it on her deerskin sling bag together with her sketchpad and colored pencils. She may as well explore for a while. She has plenty of time, the first task is not until 4 o'clock. She went out and once she was sure that the coast is clear, she sped to the woods.

She always loved the woods. Some nights, she would dream of roaming the woods in her wolf form. Feeling the cooling night breeze and soaking in the moonlight. At 8, her wolf is still asleep. Their wolves will show once a child turns twelve. That will be a momentous part of their lives. Along with their wolves came the skills that comes with it. There is even a ceremony in the school where all students aged 12 will show off their wolf for the first time in front of the whole pack. It is a very special event for a pup like her and a proud moment for their parents.

Yet, at her age she already have sharp and heightened senses. Especially her sense of smell, it is the same as that of an adult's. And at night, her vision is perfect. She can even locate anyone as far as a mile from her. She can sense enemies nearby. But she just kept this for herself. She will just show it off during the shifting ceremony and surprise everyone of her incredible wolf. Maybe, just maybe, they will accept her. Mona sighed of the thought. Another petty hope. Her granny always reminded her not to hate herself because she is special in her own ways and that the moon goddess herself blessed her birth. So much for a blessing from the goddess if it means living miserably? This must be what the adults call as irony.

She continued to follow the trail. All around her were towering pine trees and below were dried leaves and branches. The crispy crunch of those dried leaves were the rewards of her every step. These were music to her. She sniffed the air and smelled fresh, cool air. The falls is near. She excitedly run towards it. Finally, she can draw it as promised to her beloved Granny Jo. And there it was, a majestic falls of some 50 feet drop, the rocks were covered with moss, the air chilly yet refreshing, the water a sparkling turquoise. What a wonderful sight!

Without delay, she took her place beside a huge tree and started sketching the sight before her. She was too immersed in her work she forgot the time. When she finished,it was almost four. She hurriedly gathered her things and run as fast as she could to the camp house. She was panting when she reached their camp house, her face flushed. The boys were already wrestling. And the girls were seated in a circle doing something with their nails. They are ignoring her. Well, that's a first. She immediately went to the girl's room towards her cot. She gently placed her things on her bag. Not long, Tristan was barking commands to get on their feet to the camp's square. And she followed suit. She was stopped by Tristan with an arched eyebrow. She understood. "I'm fine now. I've taken the medicine and got ample rest. I'm ready for the tasks." she said brightly. He just replied a nod and gestured her to follow everyone.

"Listen Campers! The tasks are here." Ms. Kane announced touching a barrel with the Black Moon Crest beside her. The crest shows two wolves embracing a black moon. She placed her hand inside the barrel and Mona swear she heard everyone hold their breath. She picked a folded browning parchment and read:

"Obstacle Course!" the boys yelled a sound of delight while some of the girls were not so happy. The troup leaders led them to the course. It was massive with obstacles as easy as jumping on old tires to a shaky bridge, a tunnel and wall climbing. Each team are tasked to bring their flags at the last stop which is the wall. They are supposed to climb it and place their flags on the top. They have to move real quick. They only have 20 minutes to finish the task. All 10 teams get ready. At Ms. Kane's signal were the intense scrambling of feet from the campers. She came last. Her team mates were fast but she is agile as well. She moved easily in the tires, crawled up the tunnel (a dark and wet tunnel, big enough to fit the fattest boy they have which happens to be Burris), slide down (as intricate as an intestine) and fell into a net like a spider web. Went down a rope ladder, then the shaky bridge. The vines comes next (they have to swing with a vine to reach the other side) . After that was the wall.

Some of the girls were stucked, others fell while the others were moving very fast. She grabbed a nice looking vine and swung herself to the other side. She was halfway when her vine got tangled with Bruno's. "Let go rat!" he hissed. His face was very red. She just gripped tighter on her vine, determined to reach the other side. "I said let go!!" and he kicked her hard and strong in her stomach. She was positive she saw stars upon receiving that kick. Why wont Bruno try for the soccer team? He's got a superb kick! She still stubbornly holds on until she received another blow, this time it connected to her diapragm. It seemed like all air was sucked out from her body and she let go. She fell directly to the soft matress below. She was having a hard time breathing as if she had been submerged in water. She just looked up and saw Bruno successfully climbed the wall and placed his flag, a wide grin plastered on his face. What a loser! her mind screamed. But she was actually the loser. She just closed her eyes tightly and held her stomach. Now it hurts for real.

"What a start for the camp's first day! Thanks to you, we lost in the first game!" Myrtle loudly said as soon as she entered the common room. All accusing eyes were on her. She did not want them to lose. As a matter of fact, she was just a step closer to the goal if it wasnt because of Bruno. She shrugged them off and just went to their room when Paula held something up. Her sketchbook!!"Give that to me!" Mona went to Paula to grab her sketchbook. But Paula is tall for an eight-year old she held it higher making Mona jump for it. Automatically, the others were laughing. Paula throw it to Burris. He scanned it and stopped. "Little rat here is quite an artist. She's got some picture of deers? This is delicious. Oh, the falls, you sneak out to draw this did you little rat? And here's more, who's this??" "Stop it! Give it back to me!!" Mona is shouting now and ran towards Burris. Bruno pushed his leg forward making Mona trip. She fell flat on the floor. "Not so fast rat! Oh looks who's this. I bet my fur our little rat is crushing to -- Tristan!!!" Burris guffawed while the rest curiously passed the sketch around. It was Tristan's sketch. She did it unconciously after finishing the falls. Her face red with shame and anger.

"What a flirt!" Paula seized her sketchbook and ripped it in two. Not only that she went near the fire and throw it in. Her sketchbook instantly caught on fire and was slowly turning to ashes. Everyone fell silent. "That's what happens to all trash! Look! And you should know your place, Little Rat! You dont deserve anyone and that was too ambitious of you to look at Tristan! He dont even dare look at you because he cant stand your horrible appearance! What a rat!!" Paula said in gritted teeth. She indeed has the baddest blood around.

"What's this?!? Time for bed!" Tristan's voice filled the room. There she saw the pups making fun of Mona again. She was on the floor, her hair disheveled and was staring helplessly on the fire while tears were flowing in her mismatched eyes. "What have you done? Speak!" he yelled. "Paula destroyed Mona's sketchbook. She threw it on the fire..." one of the girls said timidly. Tristan looked furiously at Paula. His eyes enraged. "No, that's not true. We were playing catch and Burris did not catch the sketchbook and it landed on the fire behind him!" Paula defended herself nervously. "Right?!? " the others lookrd st each other then nodded immediately. Mona dont want to listen to all of their alibis, she is very very mad! She stood up and before Tristan can utter another word, she ran out of the cabin and ran swiftly into the dark night.

Imprinted

Mona run blindly into the night. Her fury to those bullies and her anger to herself for not fighting back creates a storm within her. She don't care anymore. She wants to go away from them. Someone grabbed her arm. Tristan!

"Where are you going? It's dangerous to be out here at this hour!" he said forcefully. "Leave me alone!" she screamed at his face and yanked her hand off his grip. "No! You will return to the cabin, now!" Tristan is not holding back either. "I alerted the Camp Masters, they will be here any minute. And if you're still here, you'll get punished!" "Then let it be. What's the difference? I'm being punished everyday anyway." she said sarcastically and move forward. "I said NO!" anger is now on his voice. She looked back at him and Tristan saw her eyes. Filled with anger and hate and sadness?? Her teardrops glinting in the moonlight. His face soften then he said in a soothing voice. "I'm sorry that they are mean to you. I know what they did, burning your book is bad. But we must come back. It's not safe here, Mona...Come on... " he held his hand to her , she just looked at it. He sighed when she did not reach for it. Tristan took her hand then pulled her carefully. She did not hesitate anymore. Realizing this is Tristan, the Alpha's son, when she froze in her steps.

"What's wrong?" Tristan asked"What's that smell? Dont you smell it?" Mona said warily. Tristan smelled the air and it was filled with a nasty smell like old unwashed grimy clothes. Tristan was all alert. "They're plenty. Six or seven... Behind the trees, coming near us." she whispered to his ear. "How did you know?" he inquired, they're back to back now, talking in hushed voices. "I can see them. They're rogues! Run!!" she said and took Tristan hand. They ran towards the camp when a filthy wolf jumped in front of them, growling. Although they have studied about them in school, this is the first time they saw it in person and tales and books did not prepare them that much. The kids were scared when two more emerged at the sides. Tristan growled back at them. These are ruthless beasts and two kids are really in grave danger. Tristan hold her hand tighter.

"Give the girl!" one rogue said"No!" Tristan said forcefully. "A brazen pup you are!" it said smirking. "Mona, you have to run! At three, you will run to the camp and call the Camp Masters!" he instructed swiftly. "What about you?" she asked worriedly."I'll distract them. I can shift, you cant. And they're plenty, we dont stand a chance. So do as I say!"Mona was hesitant to leave Tristan behind. What if something happened to him while she run to safety? "Just do as I say!" he repeated more forcefully. The rogues are closing in to them. She nodded. Tristan counted to three and she run. Tristan shifted. His wolf was as chestnut brown as his hair, and strong and big for his age but it was not as big as that of the rogues. She ran swiftly towards the camp. Not looking back. A rogue was after her and her little steps is unlike the rogue's leaps. She screamed when it reached her. It bit her arm.

"Tristan!!!! " she screamed. Tristan heard Mona's scream but three rogues were fighting him. His hindleg bitten, there were deep scratches in his back, oozing blood. Once they got Mona, they stopped attacking him.

The rogues have taken Mona away. He wont let them do so! But even if his mind wants to follow them, his body wont allow it anymore. He is not as strong as them yet. Maybe his wolf is strong but he needs a stronger body. Aside from that he is badly injured. He shifted back to his body, Mona's voice still echoing in his head, calling out his name. And then darkness.

"Rogues attacked the Camp!?!" the Alpha repeated, still in disbelief. "Yes,Alpha. One child was badly wounded, and another was taken." "Taken?" now this is new. Rogues just attacks and kills, not take hostages. It just go against their nature. "I think they just wanted the girl..." the messenger continued. "Who are the victims?" The messenger did not speak for a moment. Suspense is in the air."I said who are the victims?!""Your son, Tristan Jones and --" he jerked in his seat upon hearing it. He looked at the messenger, his brows furrowed, his heart thumping loudly."And...?""they took the cursed child - Mona Mayfield." Alpha William was stunned with the news and then he gazed at his left hand, a trail of silver thread-like light started to creep from the tips of his fingers slowly moving to his wrist? Along came a burning sensation from it.

"Do something!!!" Granny Josephine is screaming at Bill's face. "Your child was kidnapped and you are just toying with that slut!!!" she said as she stormed in his room and was enraged upon seeing him with the resident slut Vivian. Her aura is ready to kill and Bill himself felt a sudden rush of fear. Josephine will not hold back, not this time. The girl she dearly love was taken by rogues and her father is just fooling with sluts! Vivian scrambled to her feet and immediately went out of the room. "Find her Bill, please..." she pleads, tears are now streaming in her eyes, she knelt in front of him and took both of his hands."Please, Bill. Just do this for me. It will break my heart if I lose her. Maybe you dont love her. But I do. I love her as my own. Please, Bill... " she cried at him. He looked down at her for a moment and then it happened. A silvery thread creeps to his hand. They looked at each other.

"Remember eight years ago. Please remember..." she slowly said, new big tears are falling from her grey eyes.

Tristan lay sleeping on the hospital bed. His right leg was bandaged and plasters were all over his body. He was still in deep sleep that he cant feel the creeping silver thread that came out from his fingers, now creeping slowly to his wrist. "He have it too." The Alpha spoke softly to his wife. "It's a curse!" Miranda said in hushed tone"This is not a curse Miranda! How many times do I have to tell you, that girl is not a curse!""Why do I feel like you're blaming me for what happened?!" she said defensively "Because I know you did something..." The Alpha said, his eyes dark and angry. She stepped back. "I dont know anything!""If anything bad happens to that child, we will be consumed by this! Me and your son!" he showed his hand, the silver light keeps glowing as it moves slowly to his forearm. "And if it happens, we will be dead long before you realize your fault!!" he said intensely. "I didnt do anything!!" she said again, looking down at her son's hand. Her eyes worried as she bit her lower lip.

"What should we do to this kid?" asked one of the rogues. "Let's just throw her in the cliff..." suggested another. "Are you stupid?" growled the youngest one in the group. "That is just a pup!" he looked at the heap of a girl tied in both hands and feet. "Oh my Troy, have you started growing some conscience?" sneered a rather filthy rogue to him.

Troy Brooks is a tall and strong fifteen year-old. He has a long scar on his left cheek, his long jet black hair reaches his shoulders. His skin is a rich tan. He looked sharply at the man who spoke. "We received the payment. Let's leave her here and let the beasts eat her." said their leader. But something is off with Troy. He doesnt like the idea of leaving the child nor killing her.

Troy tensed up. He can hear hurried steps. Lots of it. "They're here!" he whispered.

Out of nowhere, a stunning brown wolf landed on one of the rogues, ripping its limbs apart. The others scrambled away. Troy picked the silver-haired girl and placed her on her back. Without delay, he shifted and ran as swift as the wind. Two wolves ran after him. They were running along, not far was a cliff. The girl is still unconcious on his back. One wolf tackled him so hard he was thrown to one of the trees around. The girl was tossed to the edge of the cliff. Down below was the raging waters of a river. She woke up. And when she opened her eyes and meet his, a rush of undescribable emotion filled him. But one thing is for sure, he must protect this girl for all of his life. He has found his purpose and that is right before his eyes. She's imprinted now on him. His wolf Tarsus acknowledged her, he bowed low. From this day on, Troy Brooks will live all his life to serve and protect Mona Mayfield of the Black Moon pack.

Paws thundering came in attacking him in full force. He landed just right beside the girl, his ribs cracking with every breath. He clawed the ropes that tied her. The wolves were growling at him and he returned it with a fiercer growl. He will not back down. Two wolves came into view. One very big bronze wolf and the other was black.

"Alpha William! Daddy!! " Mona shouted, excitement in her voice. She couldn't believe her eyes! Her very own father was there. He is going to rescue her!! Her heart welled with warmth.

"Stay aside Mona!" growled the black wolf. She instantly stepped aside but Troy moved quicker. He pushed her to the cliff and he jumped right after. Down to the rushing river they fell.

The Healer in Oakwood Groove

- -

Gravity is pulling Mona as swift as a bullet, and her fall did not even stop the river's raging flow. She was engulfed by the cold water and down she goes. She held her breath as long as she can but her efforts to go up were futile. The river's current was dragging her helplessly along. She's being pulled to the bottom then will bob a second later. She'll inhale and down underwater again for another minute or more. It was not long until someone grabbed her. Thanks goodness! But the amount of water she gulped is making her dizzy, add the freezing waters and the current, her head's starting to spin.

"Where is she? Where is my Mona?" old Josephine asked as she met the men charging to the packhouse. She turned to Bill. Her eyes worried yet hopeful. None of the men looked at her straight in the eye. "Alpha? Bill?! Where is she!" she demanded. "She fell. To the Moon River." Bill whispered. He dare not look at Josephine's wrinkled face. Guilt was all over his face.

Upon hearing Bill's answer, her knees turned to jelly she can't stand still. Bill supported her to one of the chairs. She felt her lungs has stopped functioning. She can't believe it! Falling to moon river is as good as dying! She held Bill's hand up in front of her and looked hysterically as if searching for evidence. It was gone. The silver trail of thread caused by the unbreakable vow was gone. She reached for the Alpha's hand as well. It was definitely gone, not a trace! Only the death of whom the promise was made will break it. Do it mean that Mona did not survive the fall?? Is she really gone?? Josephine started to wail.

Mona opened her eyes wide. She thought she's dead but she's not. In all fairness, she's feeling well as in the best she had ever in all of her eight years. Her head had some kind of minty leaves, same as her arm. She remembered being bitten by a rogue on her arm but there is not a wound in sight, only fresh scars. She sat up. Good gracious, she does not feel any pain. She removed the leaves on her body and placed it carefully on the bedside table next to her.

The room she's in is very simple and airy. The windows were wide open as the curtains made of shell danced in the wind creating a musical chime. Beside her was a wooden bedside table with a vase of fresh flowers and a small basin filled with water and leaves. An old mahogany cabinet was opposite her and also a large blurry, almost dusty mirror with intricate wooden carvings, she can slightly see her face on it. The room is filled with the smell of chamomile and lavender, calming her senses.

"I see you're awake... " a musical voice said. She turned her head automatically to its source. A very beautiful woman carrying a tray came in the room. Her very long, straight, black hair reaches to her hips. She's wearing a long dress in pale yellow with a blue string tied in a ribbon on her narrow waist. She's short and slim, but it did not change the fact that she is very pretty. She has a light, happy yet mysterious aura in her. For Mona, she is the most beautiful lady she had seen so far, almost enchanting. She smiled at her showing her pearly white perfect teeth, her eyelashes were long that complements her slightly almond-shaped purple eyes.

"How are you feeling?" she asked as she sits beside her bed and put the tray on the table. "I'm feeling good, thank you." she said timidly. "That's great." she said happily. "Here, have some porridge." she took the bowl of porridge and started stirring it. "Thank you." she accepts it and starts blowing on its contents. The lady is still looking at her and she suddenly felt insecure and lowered her head. "You are very pretty." she softly said. She blushed. Not once in her life had she received such compliment. "Thank you" she said shyly. "Who are you?" she dare asked the mysterious lady. She smiled widely, "I am Karen Sage" she held her hand to offer a handshake. "I --- I'm Mona. Mona Mayfield." she shakes her soft hand. "I know." she replied. "Nice meeting you, Mona."She looked at her with a start. How did she know her name? Understanding her startled look she just nodded and smiled. "I saw a nametag in your clothes when I washed it." she explained. She looked at herself, she's wearing a loose white dress that reaches her ankles. "Say, Miss Sage, how did you found me?" she asked warily. "I did not found you. You came to me."

It has been a week since Mona was gone. Old Josephine is still in disbelief. Her body has turned weak because of the shock and grief. She was staying temporarily in the pack house and was settled in a small room because of her condition. Bill seeing her state promised to go down river to search for Mona in the hope that she's still alive somewhere.

"I know she's still alive. She's out there, beyond the woods. She can't die. She's one tough girl..." she whispered to herself as she approched the window. "She's tougher than you think... " replied Lou, her wolf.

"You believe me, Lou?" she asked.

"Of course, Jo. And I believe in Mona too. I believe in the great things that ought are for her..." Lou replied before going back to sleep.

"That's it! I must head back home. I must prepare dinner for her. Mona might be home soon. She will be home. I will wait for her..." Lou's reply lifted her spirits. She packed her belongings and went out of the little room. She head to the Alpha's office to thank him for his generosity of keeping her even just for awhile. The door was slightly ajar and she was about to knock on the door when she heard two people arguing.

"What else bothers you? The bond has been broken. Sometimes William, you have to put a little faith in me." It was the Luna speaking. "But it doesn't feel right Miranda." The Alpha said anxiously "Look at me, W illiam..." she commanded. "I just put an end to the vow that binds you and your bloodline to that cursed girl! Since you were there to rescue and supposedly protect her, the chain of vow did not act up. You did not break the vow because you were there to take her back. Understood? It was not you who pushed her to the cliff, it was that filthy rogue! You did not cause her death! " she explained. Her voice filled with irritation.

Josephine cannot believe her ears. But the Luna is clearly speaking. She may be old but her hearing is still perfect. It means, Luna Miranda plotted to kill Mona! That poor girl!

"I came to you? What do you mean, Miss Sage?" Mona inquired. Karen stood up and moved to the dining room where she placed Mona's tray on the table. She followed her. A large china cabinet attracted Mona. Inside were bottles and jars in various shapes and sizes, filled with colored liquids. There were leaves, flowers, butterfly wings and beetles too. Karen busied herself in the sink.

"And what exactly are you?" Mona added hesitantly. Karen laughed musically. "You are such a curious and sharp kid, Mona. But don't worry, I won't harm you.I don't harm children " she turned back and busied herself again in the sink. She's washing a jar. Mona's heart pounded as she spoke.

"Then what are you? " Mona repeated. Ignoring her thundering heart."If I tell you, would you believe me?" she said, still her back to her.

"How dare you!!! Of all people! You?" Josephine shouted at the pack leaders, the Luna and Alpha. "Alpha William, you swore that day that you will do everything in your power to protect her! But you allowed your wife to kill her?? And you Luna, you are a traitor! You harmed an innocent girl!!" Josephine was enraged and with that she transformed and attacked the Luna. Both of them were shocked as Josephine charged Miranda. She tackled her and slashed her chest. She is vicious and dangerous. Miranda screamed in pain touching her chest now oozing with blood. The guards came in and captured Josephine. However, she fought them all. Tossing each guard aside, growling "You killed her!!" She's gone wild to kill Miranda. It was havoc in the Alpha's office until a sedative was injected to Josephine's spine that paralyzed her for a moment. Still, Josephine's eyes were wild with rage.

"I believe you. I promise, I wont run..." Mona even raised her hand as if pledging. "I'm just an ordinary human, Mona""But you don't smell like a human to me...""Really? What do I smell like?" Karen asked, her eyes twinkling. "I don't know. You're.... different.. ""For the humans, they call me a quack, sometimes a witch. " she shrugs. "For your kind, they call me an enchantress, a hermitress, a seer..." she said a-matter-of-factly. "But which are you?""All of it. A seer, witch, enchantress...whatever they want me to be I can become. I am a being with extraordinary abilities, Mona." she looked intently in her eyes. She approched her and hold both of her arms as she lowered herself so that her eyes were at the level with hers."Someone is waiting for you, worried and wanting you to return soon" she said. Remembering what happened, Mona shakes her head. "I don't want to return. No one wants me there. For all I know, maybe they think I'm dead and are celebrating.""I understand how you feel, but it won't last... " she said, now removing strands of loose hair on her face. "It won't last or I'll get used to it?""Listen Mona, you have been through so much. But brace yourself because there are more difficult trials ahead. It will break you but you have to be strong. It will be painful but only through pain, you will be stronger and wiser. You will make mistakes but it's okay. Because through mistakes you will learn precious lessons. You will overcome everything inorder to fulfill your destiny. Don't be afraid. You are special and blessed by the moon. You are bound for greatness..." Mona was mesmerized as she listened to her.

"Are you , by any chance, the Moon Goddess??" she said in a whisper, her voice excited, her eyes rounder than ever.

Karen laughed. "No, no, my dear. I am just a mortal called Karen Sage, the Healer in Oakwood Groove."

Josephine's Gift

"Happy birthday to you! Happy birthday to you!! Happy birthday dear Mona... Happy birthday to you..." a teary old Josephine singing that classic birthday song, carrying a pink cake with 18 melting candles. Mona Elara Mayfield turns eighteen years old today.

To their kind, it is the most important birthday and a momentous age when a wolf finally turns into a young adult and will be responsible to all of their actions. It also means that they can participate and contribute their skills and opinions for the benefit of the pack. Training will become more intense and level of discipline will be tested.

"Thank you Granny..." she said as the cake was placed in front of her. Her granny kissed the top of her head and give her a warm hug. "Now, make a wish..." she said cheerfully. "I don't have any..." Mona said flatly. "Of course you have a wish! Come on, dear..." she coaxed. "Alright..." she closed her eyes and silently uttered her wish. She blow the candles and there was a pop from a party popper. It was Troy Brooks. "Happy birthday, Mona" he greeted simply as he gave his small gift to her, wrapped in brown paper with a cute little red ribbon, he look sideways as Mona reaches for it. "Thanks Troy." she smiled to him.

Troy Brooks was one of the rogues who attacked the camp some 10 years ago and kidnapped her. She also learned that it was him who saved her in the Moon River and brought her to Karen Sage, the healer. Since then, he never wanted to leave her side and she don't know why. Granny Josephine told her that it has something to do with imprints. Another kind of bond known to their kind. According to Granny Jo, Troy was born a Guardian. A guardian is a wolf whose only purpose of living is to serve and protect their alpha for all of their lifetime. Wolves are known for loyalty and affinity to their pack, but having someone imprinted to you is another level of loyalty and is a very rare circumstance especially she is not an Alpha nor have a single drop of an Alpha's blood in her veins.

Everyone was shocked when Mona came back with a rogue in tow, ten years ago. But her Granny Jo was the first to welcome her in a bear hug when she returned. Right then and there, she knew she's loved. And one is better than none, and that matters a lot.

Everyone despised Troy and they wanted to execute him instantly even-though she tried her best to explain how he turned to be her hero. Which was ,of course, useless because nobody takes her seriously. Later on, Troy was given a chance to stay in their pack. Mona did not know what con-spired behind the Alpha's closed door during their assembly that made the Alpha accept Troy in the pack. A lot of pack members questioned the Alpha's decision but still, the Alpha's word is the law. And no one dares to go against it. Sometime after, she learned that Granny Jo, takes Troy as her responsibility, given that he saved Mona, she will have to save him too and she's willing to take him in as her son. From then on, Troy Brooks had become Josephine's adopted son. Finally, he no longer is a rogue. He has found a family.

Her father was the same. Nothing changed. He's even colder and distant to her. At least, he's not beating her anymore. Still, she's hoping that one day the tables will turn, that one day her father will acknowledge her and be proud of her. But it seems to be an impossible dream.

At 12, during the Shifting Ceremony, when everyone were anticipating that her wolf will show up on her first shifting, turned to be her worst nightmare. Her wolf just lay still and slept some more. She was frustrated she did not left her room for a week. Because of that disgrace, her father seemed to forget that he has a daughter. At the top of that, her father's friends are even questioning him if she was really his daughter or if she is one of them. Mona became the object of ridicule among her peers once and for all. Only Josephine comforted her during that frustrating phase. She said that her wolf will eventually emerge and everyone will eat their words if it happens. She keeps on telling her that it will be a magnificient wolf, that waking her wolf takes time also, that she needs more training and the sort, and some other kids experienced it too. Then she will babble her old bedtime stories about her being the moon goddess' blessed one. And somehow, it raised her hopes up.

At 16, she should have met her mate. But because her wolf is dormant, chances are, she will never meet him. And if ever, she don't think that he will accept her given her reputation and her looks. She sighed hopelessly.

"What's with that long face? It's your birthday! Cheer up, dear!" Granny Jo wake her in her thoughts. She smiled half-heartedly. Glad she have Granny who adores her and Troy on her side. As usual, her father was not in sight on her birthday. In all of her birthdays to be exact. "Here's my gift, Sweetie." Josephine said dearly. "Open it, quick." she added excitedly. She just shook her head, grinning. Josephine will always make her birthdays special by giving her gifts as simple as crayons, flower seeds, a photo frame and hair ties. But all of it, no matter how simple and ordinary, Mona valued them with all her heart. When she was 16, Josephine passed her her most precious belonging. A necklace with a jade stone. She said it's been in her family for as long as she can remember. Having no children of her own, Josephine passed it to Mona whom she treats more than a ward but her own daughter. She gladly accepts it and Mona has been wearing it eversince. She tore the wrapper and opened the box. She can't believe her eyes on Josephine's gift. An elegant off-shoulder teal evening dress was laying on the box. "It's beautiful, Gran! " Mona exclaimed. "I know, and you will be more beautiful when you wear it. Especially when we put your hair this way..." Josephine said as she lay it in front of Mona. They're standing in front of the mirror. She held Mona's long silver hair in a lovely bun."It perfectly suits you, I made it myself... " she whispered proudly in her ears, her eyes glimmering with delight. "It's perfect!" Mona replied happily. She don't know when she will wear it but it was indeed beautiful. "What do you say, Troy? Isn't Mona beautiful?" Josephine teased some more as she faced Mona to him, the latter is eating a piece of cake. Troy looked at Mona intently and shrugs. "No, Nana. She don't look beautiful... " he said plainly and faced his cake again. Mona's eyebrow automatically arched. Josephine was scolding him how tactless and ignorant he was with women, when he responded irritably.

"Because she is more than beautiful. Okay?" "She is... divine..." He added silently. His face flustered and these very lines made Mona's heart skip a beat.

That night, she sat by her window talking to the moon. She sighed again. She was about to sleep when she sensed stealthy movements from afar. As she grows up, her senses had heightened. Her instincts sharper, and her body moves quicker. She could have been a strong pack warrior only if her wolf have shown up. "What are those?" she squinted her eyes. The shadows were quite visible now. Rogues!!! A lot of them!

She scrambled to her feet and directly went to Josephine's room. "Granny! Wake up! " she knocked nonstop. Josephine was startled by the series of knocks, she opened it. "What's wrong, Mona? Do you need anything?" she asked and yawned "Granny. There are rogues! An army of rogues attacking tonight. They have entered the territory! We have to alert everyone!" Mona said breathlessly. "How come? Our rangers are patrolling our borders. They are well-trained and strong. It's impossible that they can pass through them." Josephine said calmly. "No, Gran! They're here! They have entered." as soon as she finished speaking, screams and loud explosions were heard. Children and babies were crying, men shouting commands and vicious growling filled the air. There was the sound of terror everywhere.

It startled Mona and Josephine. There was a loud banging on their door until it flew open. Five scary looking rogues burst through their door. Josephine dragged Mona inside her room and locked it. "What are you doing Gran? We must fight! We must help!" "No! You stay here and keep away from them." Josephine said as she moved towards the door. "No Gran! Don't go!" Mona stopped Josephine from going out. "Mona, I'll be fine. Maybe I am old but I'm still strong." she assured Mona. "No! You'll get hurt. You are no match to them. I hate to admit it but you are not strong as you used to be Gran. Please stay..." she pleaded. "Mona, we werewolves will never back down and age is not an excuse to stay back. We fight until the end even if it means death." Josephine said firmly. "Then let me go with you! I don't like to stay here while everyone's risking their lives!" Mona retorted "Mona, my dear, you are not yet in the position to fight. You--you are not different to an ordinary human girl in your current state..." Josephine said without looking at her. "No way! I will fight with you. I belong in this pack and I have all the right to die among them!" she yelled. "And for me your safety is more important than anything! You have protected me all my life. This time, I'll protect you. I'm sorry Gran, but you're staying." Mona is determined. She pushed Josephine to the bed and hurriedly went out and locked the door.

The rogues are destroying their house, breaking glasses and throwing things. She ran to the corridor. Troy was already fighting with the other rogues. "And so you lived...." a rogue barked behind her. She immediately recognized him as the leader of the rogues who kidnapped her. He has a wild look in his face, almost rabid, saliva dripping in his mouth. "This time I'll make sure you'll die!!!" he charged and shifted to a grey wolf. Mona picked a fallen lampshade. "You dare!" she hissed behind gritted teeth.

It charged to her and she immediately jumped sideways. It lunged to her again, as she dodged, it scratched her leg. Pain shoot to her senses like a rocket. She beats it hard and strong using the lamp she was holding it broke to pieces. She moved away from it. Wall hangings falling one by one. It lunged directly to her and she was thrown out the window. She landed on her back feeling pieces of broken glasses and debris piercing her back. It did not stop the enemy however. It was now in mid-air aiming its lethal bite to her when a brownish-grey wolf jumped colliding with the rogue.

"Granny!!!" Mona screamed. She seemed rooted on the spot. "RUN MONA!!!" Josephine yelled. A fight between the rogue and Josephine ensued. The old wolf proved to be stronger than Mona thought however the rogue was wilder than anything. It bit Josephine in the neck.

"Leave her alone!!" Mona was terrified yet enraged, she threw a rock to it and bullseye to its head. Josephine pleads Mona to run away and save herself in a voice so low she barely heard it. The rogue did not let Josephine go for it is enjoying watching Mona in pain.

"STOP IT, YOU ANIMAL!!!" she yelled furiously. Her tears were falling at the same time. She don't know how to feel anymore. The rogue just snickered and bit Josephine harder until a flesh snapped. Josephine yelped shrilly in obvious pain, her eyes still begging Mona to run as she dropped a tear for the last time.

The Moon Rises

"NOOOOOO!!!!!" Mona cried as the rogue snapped Josephine's neck and tossed her aside. Her neck bursting with very red blood and a large chunk of flesh gone she can see Josephine's bloody throat. The rogue laughed rabidly for his successful kill. Mona is filled with a different kind of fury and grief and resentment. She felt herself burning within, her bones cracking. She fell on all fours, panting, unbearable pain all over her body. One last time she looked at the rogue still laughing maniacally. "You'll pay for this!! You'll PAAAAYYYY!!!" Mona furiously screamed." Let's make them pay..." said a voice in her head. With that spoken, Mona shifted into a magnificient, slender, snow-white wolf, its purple eyes mad with fury, everyone in the vicinity was awestruck. It moved swiftly that even their wolf eyes wasn't able to follow its every movement. There is a swift wind passing through tearing and ripping limb after limb after limb. Every rogue in sight was either torn or ripped and blood seemed to suspend in the air. It was a horrific sight. After all the attackers were dead, it left out a spine-tingling howl with the bright moon in her background.

Then it walked gingerly to Josephine's side, it nudged the dying Josephine with it's slender snout. Josephine's grey eyes was transfixed to the beast's purple eyes beside her, choking blood on her mouth. In an instant, everything went still and it seems that they are the only ones around. They are transported in a place where flowers were in full bloom, butterflies flutter here and there and the breeze was sweet and calming. They are back in their bodies but they are glowing with pale yellow light. The setting sun was behind them. Josephine's back and her wolf Lou is facing the setting sun.

"Grann!!" Mona called. Josephine faced her and opened her arms. Mona instantly run for it. Josephine patted Mona's head. "Mona, I have to go..." she said lightly. "No...no... no, Granny, don't go, please. Don't leave me alone..." Mona cried. "You are magneficient, Sweetheart. I told you..." Josephine said in a motherly tone. "Granny, please... Don't leave me." Mona touched the old woman's face, as if memorizing each part of her. Somehow, Josephine's face looks peaceful and content. She smiled at Mona and look her in the eyes."I'm sorry I have to leave you so soon, Sweetheart. But from now on, you'll have to face everyday without me and it's okay. I will never abandon you for here in your heart, I will stay." Josephine wiped Mona's tears. "Don't cry now. Remember, I love you." she cajoled as she removed loose hairs on Mona's face. "I don't know if I can take it. You're everything that I have, Granny..." Mona is sobbing now. "Yes, You will be okay. You are brave and strong, you will definitely be okay. It will be difficult at first, but you'll get by...""I can't... " Mona refused at the thought "But you have to let me go. I love you sooo much but my journey stops here. It hurts that I'll be leaving you halfway but I have faith in you. In all the great things that you and you alone can do. You have to be braver to face the storms, wiser in facing adversities and trust the people who are willing to give their life to you. You are bound for greatness. Remember that... " Josephine hugged her."I will miss you so much." "I will miss you too... I love you.""I love you too, Granny. You are the parent I never had.""Your parents loves you too. Your mom and dad. Both of them. For now, I want you to promise me to give your Dad a chance." Mona nodded and smiled sadly. "I promise... "

"Josephine, time to go..." It was Lou, Josephine's wolf. "I love you, Mona. Goodbye..." Josephine gave Mona one last tight hug then let her go. She and her wolf walks towards the sun and then they were gone.

Mona came back to her senses. She looked down and she was holding Josephine in her arms, the old woman has a peaceful smile on her face. She broke down crying atop Josephine's body. Troy placed a cloak on her shoulders, gently patting her shoulders. "She's gone Troy. Granny's gone..." Mona said amidst her tears and overwhelming sadness. Troy gives her comforting hug.

Mona was not herself after Josephine died. She's sadder and does not want to talk to anyone. She stayed in her room all of the time it worries Troy and believe it or not, her Dad.

"Mona? Can I talk to you?" It was Bill knocking on her door, for the first time in eighteen years, he wants to talk to her. If it would have been an ordinary day, she would have jumped with joy but today is not the-day. She does not feel like talking, least her father who neglected her for all of her eighteen-year existence. He knocked again.

"Honey, I know you don't want to talk right now, and I fully understand how you feel. But you must not continue living this way---" Bill did not continued his words for Mona opened the door and she was staring at him, that kind of stare that seems to dig down into your soul.

"I know what I feel,Dad! And I know what to do. Just give me time to grieve... for Granny..." she retorted harshly wiped a tear from her face and closed the door on Bill's face. Bill stopped the door from closing.

"Please Mona?" Bill pleads. The first time he ever said "Please" to her.Mona stood there fo awhile until she let go of the door. "Thank you... " Bill said as he paced through the room. He sits in a nearby chair while she stood near the window. "I'm sorry about your loss, Mona. I terribly miss her too. She took care of me when I was little, and I treated her just like my mother, it hurts to believe she's gone." he said inaudibly. "I hate myself for not being there when she needs me. I hate myself even more in the thought that I was less of a parent to you than her. I know how important she is for you, I would gladly trade my life for her so I won't have to see you in this misery. Believe me Mona, I thoroughly know how it feels, I've been there before... " he said sadly. Tears were threatening to fall. "She loves you more than I do and all I ever did was hate you. Blame you for Claire's death like it was your fault she died. I don't know what to do when she died, I was not ready, I was lost. But I have become an idiot!! A self-centered asshole Mona, and you deserve to hate me..." he said cupping his face in the palm of his hands, sobbing. Mona feel sad for his father. This is the first that he is opening up his true emotions towards her. This time, she can understand why he hated her so much. She wants to hate and detest him too but how could she ever do that when it was all she ever wanted? Eversince she wanted her father to notice her. And it is happening now. "All my life, I asked myself why you can't accept me? Why you did not stood up as a father to me? Was it really hard to... love me? And here I was believing that I am a failure, a mistake, or maybe I am not your real daughter... All this years,Dad. You made me invisible. You made me feel less. You made me feel unworthy... What's with the sudden change of heart??"

"I am so sorry Mona. I really am. When you were a baby, the Luna wanted you killed because she believes you will bring chaos to the pack. But your mother stood by you, protected you with her life. The thing I didn't do. This is the proof that she loves you more than anything." Bill held her hand in front of Mona's face. She can see traces of glowing silver thread enclosing his hand. "What is that?" she asked. "This, this is the promise Mona. The vow to protect you whenever your life is threatened. And do you know what it takes to make an unbreakable bond? " he looked at her, directly in the eyes. "No..." Mona answered silently"Life, Mona. Your mother's life. She had given her life for the vow. To ensure that you will be safe. And that was the reason why I despised you. Because you took her away from me. And I am sorry....I was wrong and stupid! " he sobbed. Mona reached for his Dad and hugged him.

"I'm sorry Dad it had to happen. I had no idea... " she whispered

"No. Don't say that. It's me who should be sorry. When the attack happened, this thing here acted up that it almost burned my skin. I ignored it but you know what happened?" he paused"I saw your Mom right in my very eyes. An apparition, reminding me of the promise I made with your Mom, the vow I had forgotten.""Now I know what to do. Just give me a chance Mona. I will do better." he said holding both her hands now. "Please forgive me Mona... I realized that I could have lost you too that night and if you did, I will never forgive myself. " Bill cried even more."I am sorry, Mona. But whether you believe me or not, you are my daughter and I... love you and I am proud of you."

Mona was overwhelmed. She hugged him tighter and her heart lighter. "Dad, we can start over again. Before, I just wanted you to notice me as your daughter. And here you are now, asking for forgiveness, which before, I thought would be impossible in my lifetime. So why won't I forgive you? I had forgiven you Dad, long before you say it.. I had forgiven you everyday because you are the only parent I have and I... love you... " she said, smiling behind her tears. Bill's cry was even louder. He felt foolish yet overjoyed that the child he neglected had forgiven him and not once had held a grudge against him. That despite his treatment, she continued to look up at him. That even if he failed to be a father to her, she still loves him sincerely. Bill cried harder. As hard as the time when Claire died.

Mona felt as if a heavy veil in her heart was lifted. Finally, her moon is rising, chasing the darkness away from the corners of their hearts.

The Perfect Match

After the attack, Mona's life has somehow changed. No one dared to touch her even Paula Madison, her number one bully. Her wolf's power has frightened everyone in town and no one dared to cross her. Somehow, the results of the events are all in favor with her, given that Burris and Paula had never ceased to get in her way eversince she came back ten years ago until present. They are distancing from her with wary eyes and she's liking the peace from not dealing with them.

At home, she's undergoing adjustments now that Josephine's gone. She run for groceries and do some household chores well except cooking. It does not seem to be her strongest suit. Her produce are inedible no matter how many times she tried, meanwhile Troy shakes her off with his ever-excellent meals. So, Troy has become the chef at home. Her father proves to be doing his best to make up to her. Spending more time and teaching her some battle strategies and fighting techniques. Her father, Bill is the second-in-command in the Black Moon pack and a major strategist, an excellent commander and a wise adviser. Everyone in the pack respects and looks up to him except when he's drunk and fools around with sluts. That is the only taint in his reputation. However, Bill has been sober for months now and still going strong.

"Tristan, darling. What do you want for your birthday?" his mother, Luna Miranda asked him as they were having tea. "Don't bother, Mom." he said uninterestingly. His mother always prepares a fabulous birthday party for him and he plainly hates it. But because, he is the Alpha's son and the future ruler of their pack, he has no choice but to oblige. "No, no, never! It is also the day that we will be announcing your engagement!" Miranda said excitedly and she started blabbering about the preparations.

A wolf has a destined mate, chosen by the moon goddess especially for them, or so they say. When the right time comes, they will be revealed to each other and will be automatically bonded by the so called "mate bond". It is an irresistible bond and only few (even none) had rejected a mate before. If ever rejected, both parties will suffer a destructible heartbreak (although, the suffering is more intense to the one receiving the rejection) that is why, rejecting a mate is very uncommon to all wolf kind.

Tristan found his mate two years ago back when he was twenty and she's just sixteen. And because sixteen is too young for marriage then, they waited until she turns eighteen. After it, their marriage will follow rightafter. Maybe a couple of weeks or on a few months? He can't wait for that day to come. The moment he laid his eyes on her, he knows she's the one. He instantly fell in love with her.

She came from a prominent family and her father, Mr. Peter James, is one of the Alpha's most prized assembly member and political ally. Leizel James is a perfect match for him.

He just shrugged and said "whatever" as his eyes rolled. "I need to go Mom. I have to meet Leizel in town. She said she wants some supplies." He quickly said as he gave his Mom a peck on the cheek . "Oh sure, darling! Send my regards to Leizel!!" she said brightly and return to her event planning. This time, she's making important calls.

The entire town knows that Leizel James is his mate, and soon will be the future Luna. Although he has not marked her yet because their pack has conservative laws. Marking their mate will only happen when they are at the right age and that is eighteen, and with the proper ceremonies on top of that. In that case, he's waited too long and he can't wait to mark her so that no one else can claim her. He excitedly went out of the manor and sped to the town, driving his car.

Leizel James was standing outside Books and Bunnies. An old bookshop near the intersection. She's wearing a floral sundress in yellow, complementing her rosy skin, her long chocolate brown curls were in a ponytail. Leizel is a little short but for Tristan, it made her look cuter. She has bright little green eyes and cute pointed nose. Her smile is most mesmerizing, it takes Tristan's breath away. "Hi!" he greeted her and kissed her cheeks "Hey there!" she hugged him. She stands just below Tristan's armpits. "Have you waited too long?" he asked "No. Papa just dropped me off a moment ago. Let's go!" she said brightly. They spend time going from one shop to the next until they reached the grocery store. "I think, I'll stop by here for some basic lady's necessities..." she speaks slowly, her voice music to his ears. "As you wish my lady." he said. "I'll follow you around."

They entered and picked a basket. Leizel was walking in front of him, she head straight to the toiletries section. Leizel kept examining two bottles of lotion, comparing them perhaps? And in terms of shopping, girls will be girls! "Tristan! Hey buddy! What a coincidence!!" Henry Madison spoke behind him. He tapped his shoulders. Henry is his best buddy. He is tall and has a strong build, bronze skin and thick mouse brown hair which is cut neatly. He has prominent jaws making him look destructive and her eyes a deep blue calming his sharp features. He is Paula's older brother and unlike him, he has not found his mate yet. At age sixteen, their kind can already sense their mate, however if the other pair is not yet of age or in a rare case, the pair's wolf is dormant, they will not be able to recognize each other as mates even if they kept on crossing paths a thousand times before. Henry just laughs about it and jokes that maybe his mate is still a fetus or worst, was not yet conceived. Amd somehow, it is okay with him because it gives him the freedom to date girls he wanted. "Shopping for party needs perhaps?" he joked"No, I'm with Leizel." Tristan pointed to her, Leizel paused for a moment then smiled. "Hi, Henry!" she chirped. "Hi, Leiz..." he give her a wink. Leizel blushed. Sometimes, Tristan is jealous with Henry. But he blames it with the obsessive mate bond. Once she is marked, no one will ever touch her but him. For sure, Henry is just teasing him, and he is the greatest prankster among his peers. Anyway, he is a resident playboy and is dating girls according to his mood.

"What are you doing here?" Tristan asked."Oooh. Me? Paula asked me to grab these things. " he showed his basket and there lay bottles of liquor. "Paula? " he raised his eyebrows, Henry laughed out loud. "No, not these! But this!" he picked a lipbalm at the bottom of the bottles and held it in his face. He laughed with him. "Well, I need to check this out. See you at the party?" he said still laughing"See you, man." Tristan replied and they did their secret handshake. He was about to leave when he bumped into someone else's cart so hard, some of it's contents fell to the tiled floor. But instead of picking the fallen apples, Henry stood frozen while his eyes were transfixed to a girl picking the fallen items on the floor.

Mona make it to the grocery for some pantry supplies, she did not realize she had a cart full of supplies for she had forgotten the list Troy made for her. She just stuff the cart with anything she likes. She was about to check out her groceries when someone bumped to her cart. And just like a domino, her groceries fell to the tiled floor. She immediately picked the fallen groceries. She wants to yell to whoever was so dumb to barge in her cart like that when she was arrested with a smell so intoxicating she can't have enough. Like strawberry syrup in hot pancakes. He immediately looks up and see Henry Madison, off all people.

Henry couldn't believe his eyes. His wolf is howling and jumping with glee while screaming "mate, mate, mate!!!" in his mind. Her fragrance is so invigorating like honeysuckle and peonies, he inhaled it all at once. He has found his mate and of all people, it was Mona Mayfield, the resident freak. She looked at him and he knows right away that she's feeling the same pull of attraction.

Mona is the first to wake up in the trance. It took a lot of her courage to look away. She scampered, leaving the mess of groceries on the tiled floor and out of the store. She run as fast as she could and never looked back.

She arrived home panting, she just run a kilometer from the town center to their house. Her heart beating wild. She placed her hand in her chest to still her thundering heartbeat and breathes slowly, her sweat dripping.

Troy emerged from the kitchen, wearing an apron. "Something the matter Mona? What's wrong? You looked like an army of rogues chased you?" he asked casually, his eyebrows arching as he starts to remove his apron. "And where are the groceries?!" his arms are on his waist now. "I found him. I.. I ..I met him, Troy... " she said in between breaths. "Who did you meet?" he asked as he pours a glass of water and brings it to her. Mona just stares down at the glass of water, gazing at her reflection in the crystal glass. "My mate..."

Shattered

"I met him Troy. My mate!" Troy's face darkened as he heard Mona's words, he gripped the glass tighter it almost cracked. "Your mate?!?" surprise and disbelief are intermixed in Troy and her Dad's unison of a reply. Her father just came in, a brown paper bag in his arms. "Dad, glad you're here." Mona said as she reached for her father. "I dont know what to do, I cant think clearly. My heart beats like crazy!! I'm nervous!!" she speaks with so much anxiety. "Calm down,Honey...I know exactly what you need to do." Bill calmy said. Mona on the other hand was pacing back and forth, stressed out. "What should I do Dad? Tell me?""Bath.""What??" Mona asked in a rather high tone. "You need a bath" Bill said a matter of factly, he took a bottle of bath essence out in his paper bag and gives it to Mona. She just looks at it in utter disbelief. "You see? Rose and chamomile, very relaxing..." Bill held the product as if promoting it."Your kidding?""No I am dead-serious, Honey. Now, off to your bath.""Yeah, right."Mona said sarcastically and rolled her eyes, in this dire situation, his father is not taking her dilemma seriously. She grabbed the bottle and run quickly to her room. "Thank me later, Hon!" he laughed. "Oh, Troy, is that for me?" Bill asked pointing to the glass of water in Troy's hand. "Thank you. I'm kind of thirsty." Bill took the glass, drank its contents and put it back to Troy's unmoving hand. Bill whistles a tune as he went to his room, obviously in good spirits.

"What's wrong with you, Henry?" Paula asks her brother, who at the moment, was staring fixedly on the tv screen but obviously his mind is somewhere. They are in the sala, watching "Guardians of the Galaxy". He ignored her. "Earth to Henry!" Paula said louder and waved her hand in front of him. He blinked, as if awaken from some obscure dream. "What did you say?" immediately asked Paula, the latter laughed hysterically. "Oh, dude. Your spacing out!! Don't tell me one of your pranks went wrong? Or maybe, Alejandra dumped you! Ha-ha!!" she replied, teasing him, Alejandra is the girl he's dating as of the moment. Henry shook his head. "You bet." he said sighing. "Really? Did she dumped you? You-know-Henry Madison - the number one player in town has been dumped?! UNBELIEVABLE!!" Paula said in her nitpicky tone. "Shut up, Paula!" he yelled, glaring at her. Paula just made face to him. "Nobody dumps Henry Madison, remember?" he said irritably. "Well, if that is so, what's the matter? You don't seem to be yourself." she continued, placing popcorns on her pink lips. "I found my mate, Paula." "You did?!" suddenly Paula's eyes widen, excitement on her face. "That is great news Henry, who is she?" Henry shook his head, then run his fingers on his hair before replying silently. "Mona." "Who??" Paula said in a surprised tone. "Mona." this time louder. "What?!? Mona as in Mona-the-freak?" she was aghast "As in Mona Mayfield." he added. Shock was all over Paula's face, Henry bets that even Da Vinci will not be able to paint it.

Mona was sitting alone in her swing set in their yard. Thinking what will happen next. She felt the bond and the intense attraction that comes with it but her wolf is silent. Where did she go?

"Hey, are you there?" she asks the wolf within her. "Why don't you talk to me?" she asks more "What do you want?" it replied irritably "Why are you acting like that?" she replied sharply on her wolf's attitude. "Like what?" it said"Like you were not happy with finding our mate?" "It is just a nuisance!" it snapped"What made you say that?""Just don't set your hopes up." and then the voice is gone.

"I see it is troubling you." Troy came to where she was, holding a pack of cookies. She was in their rose garden, swinging in her old swing set. Feeling foolish and frustrated as her wolf ignored her. He sat to the swing next to hers. "Who wouldn't be?" she's still irritated. "Woah. What's with that stingy attitude? Perhaps a cookie may help." he said as he offered her the cookies. "Sorry, my bad. My wolf really has a bad attitude.""Hmm?" "She seem not to like our mate. Is it possible that your wolf wouldn't like the mate the moon goddess has given you?" "I don't know. No one can resist the mate bond they said. " he said"Hmmn. Say, have you ever found your mate?" Mona asks as she looks in his eyes. He looks away. "No.""Why not?""Because I am imprinted to you." he answered cooly"What?""Imprinted wolves has one purpose alone. That is to serve and protect our master. They can't have a mate." he looks intently in Mona's eyes. She breaks from his gaze. "That sounds bad Troy, but how many times will I tell you I'm not your master, Okay? And I don't want you to protect me. I can handle myself just fine." she said stubbornly. "But you can't stop me from doing this. It's my purpose." he said in a very serious tone, Mona can feel the intensity in his gaze. "All right then. Do as you wish. Anyway, I've been meaning to ask you this. Is it okay?" she asks to change the topic, he nods. "How did you end up with the rogues?"He breathes deeply before answering her."When I was twelve, I had a very uncontrollable wolf. He was vicious and dangerous and I can't control him. He attacked my family and killed them. All of them. My pack banished me."Mona was surprised with Troy's tale.

"The rogues took me in and I become a part of their gang. Raiding villages, accepting dirty jobs, assasinating persons and all sorts were just few of our jobs. Until I met you..." he looked intently in her eyes again. "Yeah, right." she forced a smile to him.

"Mona, you have a guest." Her father emerged from the door, cutting their conversation. She looked up to him and behind her father's back came Henry. Troy looks viciously at him and the other man to him. Her heart pounds crazily again. "I want to talk to you. ALONE. " his voice commanding, his stares wild to Troy. She looks at Troy and nods to him, mouthing it's okay. "I'll be here if you need me." Troy hissed on her ear as Henry walks directly to her. Troy leaves them alone.

"Hi." he greets her casually. Her wolf turned to him but it grunts back to sleep. ""Hi?" she greets back. "What do you need?""You." he cleared his throat. Mona's heart seems to break out from her chest. "I know, this is confusing. But we cannot do against the bond. It calls me to you." his voice sounds sexy to her. His deep blue eyes is so magnetic and his scent is totally intoxicating. "I feel it too." she said softly, inhaling.

Henry inhales Mona's scent. He looks into her bright mismatched eyes and it seems that his future is clear. Her platinum blonde hair glinting in the moonlight, he dreads to touch it. And her voice is just all it takes for him to give in. He closed his eyes to contain himself. "But I can't have you as my mate." he speaks with so much difficulty. She feels that it is not easy for him to say it. But her tears automatically fell. "What do you mean? Wh--Why?""Because..." he paused and looked up the moon. Drawing more courage. "Because I am a freak? My looks? My drawbacks??" "No. Not about that. It's more about me. I am a mess Mona, a jerk! It's unfair to someone as pure as you." Mona is crying now. "I know, I understand. I have prepared myself for this, you know. I actually have seen this coming." she draw a heavy breath. "But on the other side of that, I still hoped that this "mate-thing" will turn out good, that he will accept me for who and what I am. But we cannot force anyone to accept us, right? Especially for a girl who has been dubbed as a rat and a freak all her life. Maybe it disgusts you to know I am your mate." she said and wiped her tears angrily. "Sorry to disappoint you, but yeah, this is all you've got. " she retorted furiously. "I'm sorry. I told you, it has nothing to do with your social situation. And you don't disgust me. You are beautiful. Irresistible. Strong. And I respect you. But I am not meant for you because-- " he exhaled. " I-- I actually have someone else." She looked up at him with accusing eyes. "I've been loving her for a long time, now. My heart beats just for her." he added sincerely."And who among the girls you've messed with are you talking about?""She's not one of them. It's just a decoy. Me as a womanizer, so that no one will suspect. " he immediately answered. Suddenly, feeling defensive. " Unbelievable! What if she's found her mate? What will you do? What if she choose her mate over you??" "It won't happen. Because she has chosen me long before she met her mate.We made a promise." Mona can't believe what she's hearing. She have seen this coming but nothing compares to the pain she's feeling right now. The actual heartbreak is not matched to what she thought it will feel like. "That is why I came here to ask for your forgiveness to what I will do." he said with finality, pain reflected in his eyes."I'm sorry Mona, but I love her above anything else. You deserve someone who will completely accept and love you." he has tears on his face now. She just looked up at him with pleading eyes. He took her hand and with closed eyes, he uttered"I, Vince Henry Madison, rejects you, Mona Elara Mayfield, as my mate."

Hearing this, Mona heard a sound like glass breaking.Realizing it was her heart, completely shattered.

The Next Queen

It is really happening. Henry Madison rejected her. She bowed her head and cried like she never did before. The pain is too unbearable for it. Henry too is in pain. Both parties will be affected by breaking the mate-bond and the pain is not funny. "Mona... I'm so sorry. But please---please let me go... " he whispered crying. Henry sounds pitiful, who would have thought that this one-of-a-kind man whom every woman begs for attention is now begging her just to let him go? Mona clearly understands Henry's situation. Having such courage to break the mate-bond to follow his heart is rare. She have no choice but to let go. "I, Mona Elara Mayfield, accepts this rejection from you, Vince Henry Madison. May you find happiness to wherever your heart will lead you... " she whispered, restraining her sobs. He hugged her and whispered thanks to her ear. "I wish you the best." she said as she looked at his eyes. "Thank you..." he murmured. She can't take it anymore, she left him and ran to her room. There she wept bitter tears.

"I told you not to raise your hopes up." her wolf pronounced at the back of her mind "Why did you not stop him?!?" Mona muttered angrily. "He is wounded too, Mona. His wolf by far is more hurt. Besides, you are not invested to him yet and it's a good thing because the pain from the broken bond will not last long. He don't deserve us." her wolf lectured her sternly. "Can you feel it too? This misery?""Yes of course! I am not numb, Mona. I can feel the effects of broken bond too. So gather yourself now. You had enough crying to last you a lifetime. We will never be crying again, remember that." It proclaimed with finality and conviction

Mona did not know what time she fell asleep last night. She just woke the next day with the sun's rays hitting her face. There was a knock on the door. "Mona, time for breakfast!" Troy uttered in a loud voice, his knocks seem to break the door. Mona lazily rise up and opened the door. "Hold up tough guy, I'm awake." she yawned in front of him. "What time is it?""Past eight? Look at you! " he exclaimed. "What?!?""You look like a piece of shit! Go, do something with your face, take a shower, whatever! Quick!" He is pushing him to her bathroom. "The heck,Troy??""This is heck Mona. You are!" he said, facing her in the mirror, his strong grip on her shoulders. Her reflection shows a very stressed face, dark circles under her puffy eyes, sagging eyebags, dry skin and chapped lips, not to mention her hair like a bird's nest. "Go and fix yourself!" he demanded as he picked and throw a towel on her face. "Yes, Mom!" she rolled her eyes at him. "Get down when you're done. Breakfast's ready." he announced before leaving her room. Mona can still feel the ache of yesterday. "You will do just fine, heart. It's okay." she murmured, massaging her chest.

Henry lay awake all night. He's still in bed, his eyes fixed on the ceiling. He can't believe that he rejected his mate. Maybe he is the first man in their town's history to ever reject a mate. He grunted and turned sideways. It was Mona Mayfield anyway, the town freak and the silver rat, the cursed girl. Paula was the happiest when she learned that she rejected Mona. She did not even bother if he will be affected by it as long as he gets rid of her. She emphasized that she will never accept her as a sister-in-law! No wonder, Paula have never liked Mona, like EVER! But his heart is mad and his wolf madder at him. Craig, his wolf is not talking to him since he rejected her. He was totally head-over-heels with Mona's wolf, and is determined to ignore him. He keeps howling in his head and giving snide remarks at him making him feel insane. Henry just hopes that Craig will be as understanding as Mona. If only he had not given his heart long ago, he would have taken Mona. She has an air of confidence in her and a heart so pure. Amidst her cruel experiences with the people around her, she still keeps a straight and brave face on, and forgives them. If it was him in her position, he would have hated the world. Her wolf is something to be feared too. It was strong, unforgiving and somehow dark, he even trembled when he saw it during the rogue's attack in their town. He must face this. He can go on just like Mona Mayfield. Besides, there's a party he needs to attend. "Henry? Son!" his father knocks on his door. He opened the door and saw his father, looking seriously at him. "Mr. Mayfield is here... " his father announced.

"Where's Dad?" Mona asked while munching her pancakes swimming with strawberry syrup. Now she's reminded of Henry again because of this scent, she feels her heart aches."At the pack house with the Alpha." Troy answered casually. "What time did he leave?" "Just a little before seven? He mentioned he's dropping by the Madison's too." he continued eating his fill. She almost choked when she heard "Madison". "What? Why did he went there?" she asked, her voice a little high pitched. Troy just raised his eyebrow. "Maybe to ask why he did it to you..." he responded silently. Mona averted her gaze and focused on eating.

"NO! No! No! Don't place those flowers there!" Miranda shouted to the maid, "It would look better on that side." She instructed. She has been very busy in the preparation for Tristan's birthday. It will be tomorrow evening yet she is starting to be stressed, she can see fine lines in the corners of her eyes as she accidentally saw her reflection in the plates the maid is polishing. "This can't be!!!" she squeals observing her face closely. "I need to go to Dr.Jensen now!"she told herself. "Bruce!!!" she called her personal assistant, which the latter attended very quickly. "Book me an appointment to Dr. Jensen, NOW!" she commanded. "Yes, Luna." Bruce bowed and immediately took his phone and made a call. "Appointments made, Luna. She will see you in half an hour." Bruce reported. "Great. Miss Jean, can I have a moment?" She called the attention of a middle-aged woman Jean Rogers, her event coordinator. She is busy checking something in her tablet. "Yes, Luna?" Jean approached daintily. "Please take over from here. I have an appointment with Dr. Jensen today.""You can count on me Luna." she said firmly. "Well, I expected to. I want this event to be perfect! See you around." as Miranda turned her heels and went to her room for a change of outfit. Bruce followed her as the servants around bowed to her as she passed by them.

"Hello there, pretty!" Bill called Mona. She is tending her roses, a box of fertilizer beside her. She just rolled her eyes to him. Bill is glad that their father-daughter relationship is progressing very nicely. He is grateful that Mona has such a kind and forgiving nature, Bill can't help but curse himself for being an idiot."What's up, Dad?" she smiled at her. He hardly notice this before but whenever Mona smiles, he can see Claire. She looks like her, the shape of their eyes and face, the nose and that very smile he fell in love with. "What's with that stare?" she remarked. "Nothing." he shrugged. "I have something for you...""What is it?""This!" he showed her a blue envelope with the Black Moon Pack crest. "What is that?" Mona inquired "Open it." Mona took the envelope from her father's hand, she flipped it over and saw writings in italic,

Mr. Bill Mayfield and familyYou are cordially invited

"This is an invitation... " Mona whispered. She opened the flap and saw the card. "It's for Tristan Jones' twenty-second birthday and engagement party.""Yes, you are correct! " Bill said, very pleased."I don't want to go!" she said and returned the invitation to Bill's hand. "Don't be silly! This is a grand event, not only it is the young master's birthday but also his engagement! We can't miss this kind of event..." he explained robustly."I'm not interested, Dad." she replied. Actually she's apprehensive about it. If she go, it will be the first time she will join a grand event like that in her life. She never attended a party before, much more with this grand event? She will look like a country bumpkin if ever, she'll just embarass her father more. "No, Dad. I don't want to." "But honey, everyone in the pack is expected to witness this. Come on... "Bill pleads "You have been sad over Henry, and I had given him a lesson already, this party will distract you from the effects of the broken bond and --""You taught Henry a lesson?! " it seems like it was the only words Mona had heard "Yeah, but he's fine now. We have amazing healing abilities you know, for sure, his pretty face will be back to normal in no time... ""But you hurt him!" she retorted on disbelief. "Yes yes. Sorry. Okay? But what he did was unforgivable. Besides, no one can hurt my Mona without paying a price. No one. " He looked intently in her eyes. "So, we will go to the party tomorrow evening. And that's final." he left her. Her jaw dropped. "And oh, Troy can come too!" he said when he met Troy in the door, the latter bringing a tray of snacks.

Mona has never been so nervous before. Today, her heart seems like to jump out of her ribs. Her father had hired an entire glam team to glam her up for this event. She refused it but her father insisted that she have to look her best, given that she will be his muse for tonight. She argued no more and just thinks that this is one of his ways to make up with her.

Bill is party ready. He is wearing a white tuxedo, and a rose in his lapel. At his age, he still is dashing. But to all the parties he's been, this is the first time he will bring the daughter he neglected for so long. He hopes that this will be his saving grace.

Mona came down the stairs and Bill couldn't recognize her at first. She is beyond beautiful. She is wearing the teal dress Josephine had given her on her eighteenth birthday, her hair was in a lovely and elegant braid, her creamy shoulders exposed in her dress. Bill has never been so proud. He saw Troy in the corner of his eye and just like him, he was awestruck. "Hi Dad." she greets him and she nods to Troy's direction."You look heavenly, Mona... " Bill said as he took her hand. "Well, the two of you looks dashing as well." she winked at Troy. "One moment, this will complete your look." Bill took a diamond necklace in his pocket and placed it in her neck. "This is your Mother's. Now, it's yours to keep." He said as teary-eyed. "Now, you are perfect! " he exclaimed. "Thanks Dad!" she hugged him. "It's beautiful..." her father nodded appreciatively. "Let's go."

The party was, as expected, fabulous. The decorations were prime and the foods, excellent! As soon as Bill's company entered, everyone's attention turned to them. They can't help but admire Mona's exquisite beauty. "Dad, I think they don't like me here. They keep on staring." she whispered to him"No Honey. They are just admiring you.." he replied and squeezed her hand gently. She saw Henry among the crowd, looking at her passionately. She looked away.

The party started, dancing commenced, foods and drinks were in abundance. Later that night, was the official announcement of Tristan's engagement. Tristan head straight to the mic and thank everyone for coming and for the birthday wishes. She haven't seen Tristan in a while since he graduated in the school. He started his training for the pack and for his Alpha duties. He is ravishing in his red tuxedo but he looks somewhat off, like angry and sad at the same time. But maybe, he is just having a severe stage fright.

"This night" he began his speech , his mother looking very proud and elegant as always, has a wide smile plastered on her face. "is not only a celebration of my birthday, but a celebration for the beggining of a lifetime. And I want everyone to witness this momentous event in my life" he continued.

"Ladies and gentlemen, may I have the honor to present the next Luna of the Black Moon Pack... " he paused again and looked at everyone's faces in the crowd and smiled to them. Everyone held their breath in anticipation. He swept through the crowd once more and stopped in her direction, a sudden gush of cold wind seems to sweep on her body.

"The next Queen, Miss Mona Elara Mayfield."

When Love and Hate Collides

A spotlight was turned to Mona, she was actually breathless. The excited clattering before the announcement has ebbed. Only silence and bated breath. He walked slowly towards her. His eyes were fixed on her, dark and dangerous. She don't like the feel of it yet his presence excites her. He stopped in front of her and offered his hand. She peered at his father and saw that he looked appalled. "Mr. Bill Mayfield Sir, if you may..." Tristan broke the spell, her father was back on his feet and gazed at Tristan's hand. He smiled sheepisly as if a little boy caught stealing cookies in the cookie jar. He placed Mona's cold hand to Tristan's waiting hand, he then placed it in his arm then shakes hand with him. "Thank you, Mr. Mayfield. I will take care of your daughter for all of my life and the next. She will be treated with outmost care and above all, she will be loved..." he uttered very slowly. His lines made her heartbeat quicken. She seek for Troy and he was not looking well. He looked furious but was restraining himself. Tristan slowly took her back to the stage. She saw the crowd's disapproving glare, especially that of Paula. They passed by Leizel James, the supposed-to-be fiancee of Tristan. What happened to them? She looks stunning as usual but it wont hide the sadness in her eyes. Did she cry? Did Tristan broke their bond too?? He looked at the man beside him and found him rather sexy, she scolded herself. Henry was looking at them as if he had ingested something foul.

Luna Miranda approched Tristan and murmured harshly in his ear "What's this madness Tristan?!? Have you gone out of your mind?" her gaze can pierce through a solid wall like concentrated laser beams. "Maybe I am." he said mockingly. Seriously, what's wrong with him? Mona was racking her brains for an answer.

The Alpha steps up and applauded. He went into the mic and spoke in a very cheerful tone. "This is great! Just great! Everyone, our next in line, My son and heir, Tristan Jones and his enthralling bride-to-be, Mona Mayfield!!" he laughed then applauded, he seemed very pleased or maybe he was just acting. As of the moment, Mona is very confused. Everyone in the room followed with hesitant claps and conniving murmurs. Then the music played.

Tristan took her to the dance floor, never in her life she had been this close to any man, his heat radiating making her face blush. He placed his hand on her narrow waist and holding the other. He was looking down at her, boring holes deep in her head. Maybe trying to look into what goes on with her mind. "Why don't you look at me?" Mona swears his voice is very sexy. She calmed herself before meeting his gaze."I am still processing what is happening to us..." she replied softly"Isn't it clear yet. I choose you as my bride.""You can't just do that!" she protested, she removed her hands from his touch. "Yes I can. Now don't make a scene." he took her in dancing position again and they continued to sway in the orchestra's slow music. "You are making a scene! Not me! What would Leizel say? Her family? Her feelings---" Mona rapidly said in hushed voice but Tristan cut her out. He suddenly pulled her closer to him, she can already feel his raging heartbeat and when she looked at him again, she saw fires of fury in his eyes. And disappointment? "Don't you dare speak her name again!" he hissed harshly in her ear, Tristan is angry. She tried to push him but he is stronger he kept pinning her to him. "Let go,Mr.Jones. You are not yourself. You have to think this over. Clear your head a little bit, don't drag me with your misery. I have been too many miseries before, I have no plans of adding to it." she told him, pulling herself away. Tristan hold both her arms tight it hurts. "No lady, you will be my bride! You cannot reject me. No one will reject me ever again!" he hushed harshly on her face, he is dark with fury. "Let go! You're hurting me!" she saidSomeone grabbed Tristan's arm, it was Troy. Looking fierce and ready to fight, Henry emerged too. "The lady said let go." Troy said, his voice threatening. They looked at each other's eyes, sizing each other up. "Don't tell me what to do, Rogue!" He spat back to Troy using his very domineering Alpha tone. He looks at Mona and lets go of her. Troy immediately grabbed Mona to him and they moved away from the curious crowd.

"Why? What's wrong with me? Have I done something wrong? Did I upset you? Am I not enough?!" Tristan glared at Leizel, his voice breaking. Tristan feels like crazy. Very crazy. He can't make sense what had transpired just before the announcement of their engagement. He feels dumb and broke at the same time. Leizel James, the girl he wanted to share his life with, wants to reject him.

Leizel asked him for a walk because the crowd in the Manor was suffocating her, as she said. Maybe she was gathering her courage to break up with him. "I'm sorry Tristan. You are perfect. You are great man but I must break up with you..." she said in her lovely voice. "You did not do anything that will upset me, nothing at all.""Then why?" he said, almost a whisper"Because I'm in love with someone else..." she confessed, her head bowed down and her shoulders are shaking from her sobs. "That is bullshit! You told me you love me! Have you not?" Tristan is yelling now. Good thing, the music from the party drown out his voice. "I do. I do love you but ---" he did not let her finish."But you love someone else? How could it be?""I loved him even before I met you. I love him until now..." Leizel is choking with tears."You betrayed me!" he accused "I never thought you'll be a two-timer, Leiz. I looked up and respected you. Put you in the pedestal and yet, you have the guts to betray me??" he screamed at her. She just cried some more. "No-no, Tristan. I did not betray you. I did not ---""And what do you call it? Huh? Loving someone else while you are my girlfriend? But you are not just my girlfriend! You are my mate!!!""Believe me, we stopped when I met you and learned you are my mate. We gave each other up to fulfill the mate bond. So I never really betrayed you.""Still, you love him right? You did not wholly gave your heart to me because you love him!" "I'm so sorry Tristan. I am so sorry..." Leizel is on her knees now, sobbing so hard it breaks his heart to see her that way. "I will not do it. I won't let you go. Leizel, I love you so much. I have never loved this deep before and I will fall apart if you break the bond. " he pleads her. "You have to, Tristan. Or else... " she stood up and meet his hurt eyes. "Or what?"" I'll die. Six years ago I made an unbreakable vow with him. Back when I was twelve, I already knew that he was the one for me. And I to him. We made it because we are so sure of ourselves, even when we were young, we knew that what binds us was love and it never changed until now." she explained."I don't care what people will say, and I am tired of following my family, their dictates on how I should live my life. This is my life! I wont let them dictate me now. This time, I will follow my heart. I will listen to what it says. And that is to break this bond and love the man I made a vow with freely and with all my heart..." she speaks sincerely and with conviction, her tears like pearls rolling in her perfect face. "And if you truly love me Tristan, you have to let me go..." she said this softly, inaudibly."That is so selfish of you Leizel... So selfish... " Tristan cried. "Tristan, you are one great man and one day, you will lead our pack with pride. But I don't see myself beside you. You deserve a woman who will match your fire, your will and your strength. It isn't me Tristan... " she said as if coaxing him. "Why can't it just be me? I promise I will be better. I will give you everything..." he begged, Leizel just shook her head. "Tristan, thanks for trying but I can't tell my heart what to do, it has a will of its own. My mind knows that I am wrong but my heart screams I am doing it right. I have been in love with him since I was twelve and nothing has changed... I am so sorry. I really am. He is all I need." "I love you so much it hurts like hell, Leizel. But I will do it. For you. All I want is your happiness, even if it means letting you go. Let's do it.""Thank you. I will forever be grateful to you Tristan...""Let's do it before I change my mind."He ordered, choking emotions in his throat. Then she began the chant, and with a heavy heart, he complied. Their bond has been broken. "Leizel, I won't forget you. I will forever yearn for you." he said, touching her face. "Me too. My wolf will never forgive me but it's okay. I know I can handle whatever the consequences be.""Please be happy. And if ever he hurts you, please come back to me." Tristan said, still holding on to his last straw of hope. "He will never do that. But if ever, I will... " she promised. "You know, I want to be him. That man you willingly give your life to, the man who owns your heart. I want to be him...""You are different from him. You are fire and he is rain. But you will do well, you have the Alpha's blood in you. Everything will be fine. I wish you to find the woman you deserve. She's just out there waiting" she said calmy. "I love you." Tristan whispered, she did not replied. Tristan kissed her lips for the last time as a tear fell from his eye. He is leaning on her forehead. Breathing her in for the last time. "One last question, Who is he?" he whispered with eyes closed. Leizel went in to kiss him on the lips, looked at his eyes and smiled. There was a sparkle in her eyes and her words seemed to dim his world.

"It is Henry. Vince Henry Madison. He is my man...." Upon hearing this, Tristan's world crumbled.

Claiming the Alpha's Bride

Mona could not believe what has happened in the party. She never wanted to be in the spotlight, worst be engaged in a blink of an eye. And not just to any ordinary man but to the heir of the Black Moon Pack! She can imagine herself as shocked as Pia Wurtzbach way back the 2016 Miss Universe tilt. She must have looked epic. Her head suddenly felt light and dizzy, she lay in her bed restlessly and annoyed.

"Don't you like the new mate?" after a long time she finally spoke to her in her superbly sarcastic tone -her wolf, Thalia. "It doesn't feel right, Thalia!" she snapped at her. "But why? He possessed strength beyond measure, prime intelligence, reliable abilities and a future Alpha and on top of that...handsome... sexy... and hot. " she can understand Thalia was already attracted to Tristan and his wolf but she was not as pleased with her right now."Stop it! You're not making any sense!!" she said hotly to her. "Don't you lie to me girl, because I can sense it. You already liked him before I do. Even before I came to you... So what's with the fuss? Not everyone gets the chance that you get..." she murmured teasingly, then she remembered ten years ago. When Tristan tried to save her from the rogues. How he risked his life to protect her during that unfortunate night. When she returned, he remained neutral and casual at her when everybody else were making fun of her, stopped the bullies and told them to leave her alone. Back then, she wanted to believe that Tristan is different from the rest. Now she don't know. She sighed. "See? You want him. Admit it, don't stop yourself, he is all yours now." Thalia nudged her in her mind. Still im her teasing tone "Shut up Thalia! You are only making things worse! I'm going to sleep!!" she shut her up, sometimes, Thalia is great in adding salt to your wounds. This time is one of those. Mona can still hear Thalia's teasing laughters in the back of her head. She just closed her eyes firmly and covered her face with her pillow.

Light rays are hitting her face. Maybe she forgot to close the windows or draw down the curtains. Whenever that happens, it is game over to Mona. She has to be awake! She stretched her hands, her eyes still closed. She waited ten seconds before opening it. There she saw the window. Gosh, she really did forgot to close it last night. But there is a silhouette by the window and is drawing near to her bed. "Good morning, Sweetheart. " a sexy voice said. Her eyes bulged out of its sockets seeing Tristan in front of her. She screamed at the top of her lungs.He is wearing a white fitted top, his sexy torso is almost visible. Her heart is under attack. Suddenly her door flew open, there came her father and Troy, worried and ready to fight."What happened Mona?!" her father speaks first, looking around and then to Tristan who was now leaning on the window again. "Nothing Dad, I was just shocked to see him in my room." she said trying to calm herself"We thought that he is violating you!" Troy added in a protective tone. "What did you say, Rogue?" Tristan said as he looked angrily at Troy. "Wait. Troy, Dad, it's fine. I'm fine. Really. And you Mr. Jones, what are you doing in my room?" she scold Tristan. "What else? I'm here to collect my bride." he replied straightly, not a single blink in sight.

"This can't be!! Do something William! I don't want that cursed girl be part of our family, MY FAMILY!" Miranda is yelling at William. She was very upset with Tristan's ploy last night and she could not believe that her husband just let it happen. The Alpha on the other hand just shakes his head. Early in the morning and his wife is already bursting with anger. She never really liked Mona eversince she was born. She believed that the girl is a living curse and must be eliminated. "It's time that we acknowledge Tristan's decision. He is in the right age now, soon I will pass him the Alpha duties. We have to trust him. Besides, how many times have I told you that Mona is not cursed. She is just an ordinary girl and it is not her fault that she was born that way. She is perfectly fine and I guess, perfect for our son." he said calmly to her. However, what he said just adds fuel to Miranda's anger "Perfect? Or maybe because she is Claire's daughter!" she spat at him. His eyes met hers and hers were nothing but furious. "You think I don't know William? You think I am dumb? I know exactly how you felt for Claire! You and her had a thing in the past right?" she is really angry now. "We have been through this before, Miranda. What's past is past." "Yes, it is in the past and you are still living in it. Do you think I will have a chance over her if it was not the mate-bond? No. Never! Because the only person in your heart was Claire! Dont dare deny it William!!" she is pointing at him, her vent up emotions now exploding in a burst of jealous flames. "I won't deny that I loved Claire. But I let her go even before our mate-bond appeared. And as you can see, she has been happily married with Bill. And I to you.""Were you?" Miranda eyes were brimming with vengeful tears. "What?""Were you happy to be married to me?""I am and is still happy with you. The moon goddess chose you for me. We were made for each other...""Then why? Why didn't I feel it? Your happiness whenever we're together? Instead I feel like I am not enough? Why do I always have to prove myself to you? Why dont you look at me the way you looked at her? And why the hell are you still keeping a picture of her?!" she yelled her last question "All these years, you never let me in. She married someone else, she died and all but I never won against her, not once! I may have became the Luna, but I never owned your heart. She did." she said trying to stop her tears from falling, full of reproach. "Miranda... What are you saying?"

he cooed at her, "It's final. I won't take her as a daughter-in-law. I won't take a bitch that will remind you of Claire!!" she turned her back and left him dumbfounded.

"Take me? Are you crazy??" Mona stood up from her bed and paced to the bathroom. "I am not going with you!" she firmly said. After she said this, 3 maids came in, carrying suitcases."Please take all her belongings. Quick!" He commanded to the maids "Yes, young master!" they answered in unison and immediately opened her closet. Mona haven't got the time to react for everything was moving too fast. She just looked at her father sighing. "Just give me an order Mona, and I will throw them out of the house."Troy said, still glaring at Tristan. Bill just nods to Troy, signalling him everything was fine. "Young Master, with all due respect. My daughter is still in shock from last night's announcement and taking her with you immediately is fairly shocking to her." Bill started, his voice fatherly and respectful. "Mr. Mayfield, sir. Or should I start calling you father?" he looks at her. He cleared his throat before speaking again. "I don't see any problem with this. You know the traditions well, do you?""Er-yes. But can we give Mona a little more time to digest everything?" "No. She will get by. Continue packing." he said cooly to the maids which then again answered in unison as if trained dogs. "And you," he is referring to her"Fix yourself. We will be leaving in ten minutes." he commanded before leaving the room. She was dumbfounded and helpless. "Dad?!? What will I do?" she said helplessly"Just do what he says.Better not to go against an Alpha's temper." her father commented.

It was not until thirty minutes after she was able to completely gather herself together. Tristan looked at her very impatiently, she can clearly see his nostrils blaring while she was climbing down the stairs. "What took you so long?? We are late!" he said reproachedly. She hugged her Dad, this engagement thing is such a nuisance. It was not long when she and her father had started to work on their relationship and yet she will be removed from him too soon. "I will come with you." Troy blurted, a backpack in his hand. "You are not invited, rogue!" Tristan rebuked. "I am not talking to you, Alpha's son. I am talking to Mona!" he retorted. Mona can feel bad aura surrounding the two. "Actually, Young Master. Troy will stick with Mona. Whether you like it or not. He's kinda imprinted to her. I guess you know what happens to imprints if they can't fulfill their purpose..?" Bill chimed in, his tone friendly. If ever imprints were not able to fulfill their purpose they become savages. And Mona don't like Troy to become a savage, given he is the only friend she got. "He will come with me." she said firmly in Tristan's face. "I am not going anywhere if he is not with me."

"Whatever!" Tristan turned his back angrily. "Don't worry about me Sweetie, I can handle myself. Besides I'll see you in often. I am second to the Alpha right? So, I can linger around." he winked at her. "And Troy, please do your duties well. I am counting on you." Bill said in a very serious tone. The two men locked eyes and seemed to communicate silently. "Yes, sir!" Troy firmly said.

The car's blaring horn signalled the end of their farewells. She left her father and walked towards the car. She looked back at him smiling wistfully as he waved her goodbye. She waved back at him. Mona never thought that it would be the last time she will see his father.

The Black Moon Manor

They arrived in the Alpha's private Manor after a twenty-minute drive. The residence is an old, huge, pitch-black Victorian Manor with its tailored gardens and magnificent topiaries. This has been the Alpha's residence since the Black Moon pack was established a half of a millenia ago. It is located a mile from the heart of the town, whereas the Pack House, at the same time, the Headquarters are in town. They passed by the massive brick packhouse, where the Alpha and her father are doing their pack duties. The packhouse serves as the Town hall, complete with amenities in case of large gatherings (where Tristan's grand birthday bash and epic engagement occured). The Black Moon Council also held office there, their High Priest and the Great Elders, all convene in the PackHouse in times of meetings, assemblies, and conferences.

In this modern year, their pack is prized for strictly upholding old-age traditions, rules and virtues. They have not done any amendments to the olden laws with which she was torn in the moment.

One of which, (primarily that covers of a soon to be Luna) states that once a woman was formally engaged or was chosen as the Alpha's bride, she will be removed from her family and will start living with his future mate. They will live under the same roof but on separate rooms to protect each others purity.This will also serve as a challenge for the couple to restrain themselves from the tempting presence of each other and check their level of responsibility and obedience to given protocols. During the duration, they will be trained according to social, political, moral and family standards. The Bride-to-be, will be educated by the Luna herself while the groom will continue his daily routines and trainings. Until such time, the pair are ready for the next ceremonies. There are two official ceremonies, the wedding officiated by the High Priest and the marking/union ceremony led by the Great Elder, usually the latter event will occur during a full moon where the Moon Goddess' power is at peak. Basically, the Great Elder will do some rituals and offerings to the Moon Goddess so that she will bless the marriage. Mona now realizes the impact of these traditions especially to her.

These laws and traditions have been taught to them at school, Mona is a relatively attentive student but she was not always at her best.   Either she was too bothered or too bullied to listen. In addition, reality is far too complex from theories. Mona just wished to go back to her old home. Her life that has started to lighten has turning in an unpredictable twist once more.

The Alpha and Luna was waiting for them along with the many servants of the Black Moon Manor. As they stepped down from the car, an echoing greeting from them meet her. The Alpha met them happily while the Luna seems to be unwell. Maybe she had swallowed something bitter. Especially when Troy emerged behind her, the Luna's face looks even more grim.

"Mona, welcome to the family! And Troy, it's good to see you again." The Alpha, as good-natured as he is, offered his hand to Troy for a shake. Troy immediately accepted his hand and shake it gently.

"You are also welcome in our home." The Alpha smiled genuinely to both of them. His cheer is utterly contradicted by his wife's grimance. Either way

, the Alpha's greetings lifted some of her worries, still, the Luna makes her nervous. Her piercing glares and her evident dislike to her. Suddenly, her childhood demons are slowly creeping to the surface. She reminds herself to be very careful especially around her and keep her cool.

She was brought to a large bedroom where the dominating colors are red and gold. Her bathroom is as big as her old bedroom in her home, she even have her own bathtub the size of a bed, the furnishings in the room are elegant and she loves the four poster bed covered in red and gold. Large windows in scarlet drapes, plush carpets so soft as fresh snow, a velvety red couch with gold trimmings and a crystal chandelier above. Troy was in the next room from hers. It was as large as her room and the colors are all moss green, from the drapes down to the carpet. All in all, the Black Moon Manor screams grandeur and timeless elegance, she felt so out-of-place.

"Miss Mona", a maidservant called her, "the Luna needs you in the dining hall." she said politely.

"Yeah, let's go." Mona smiled at the girl as she replied and nudged Troy.

"The Luna also said that the gentleman should stay where he is." she added, referring to Troy. He was about to oppose when Mona hold his arm and mouthed it's okay.

"Wait for me here..." she said brightly to Troy. The latter nodded. The maidservant brought her into a dining hall. It was large and the furnitures glisten everytime it catches light. The centerpieces are quite a sight and above all, another grand chandelier hangs above the dining table. Maybe the Jones loves chandeliers.

"Sit." a cold voice echoed in the room disrupting her thoughts. The Luna was sitting in the top chair. Untouched food lay in front of her. She meekly went near her and sit in the nearest chair.

"You called for me Luna?" she asked hesitantly. "Do you need something from me?"

"Yes. In fact, I need to give you clarifications and some pointers... " she sternly said with her perfect brows arching.

"Yes, Luna. What are those clarifications?" Mona felt her scrutinizing gaze from her head down to her feet, as if her gaze can penetrate through the mahogany table to see her feet. Still, she felt shivers climbing up and down her spine with her every cold stare.

"I don't like you for my son, and I don't like you as a person..." she tensed up when the Luna uttered these words with conviction. She was speechless. All her life, she was used on being judged and the Luna's remarks are just some icing in her cake.

"You are not even his mate chosen by the goddess and for all I know, he is still pining for Leizel and is just using you as a cover-up." she continued coldly, even her tone is full of sarcasm and dislike. Seriously, how can you dislike people even without knowing them well? Is this the meaning of that cliche "first impression lasts"? Clearly, Mona is not having a great first impression of her too.

"What do you mean, Luna?" she quietly said, choosing her words.

"Tristan loves Leizel more than anything but she chose another man over my son! She is the perfect girl for him and we could have made amends if only you did not show up! You ruined all my plans!" she was blaming her for her failed plans as if she stole Tristan from Leizel. Her face now is already red, not from shame but from her restrained anger.

"But Luna, with all due respect, I was also taken by surprise during that night. I was shocked that he picked me over other eligible girls around. And to clarify, I did not do anything that caused them to break their bond.

It was their decision. Besides, I am just acquainted with your son, nothing more. " she was surprised of herself that she was able to say all of it calmly.

"Why don't you ask your son on why he do what he did before blaming me of something I have no idea of." she added. The Luna's eyes glinted dangerously, her alarms can blaring on her.

"If there is nothing more to say, may I be excuse now?" she stood up, if she don't respond at the count of three, Mona will walk out. And three! She was about to leave when she speaks, this time, in a very chilly tone.

"Not too fast girl. I would like to remind you that I am the Luna of the Manor. What I say is the law here. Don't be too confident, you and Tristan are not married yet. Therefore, don't feel entitled. Follow every word I say and we won't have a problem. Above all, hold your tongue and don't talk back to me, you are not on my level. Remember what you are!" she leaned closer to her ear. Very near she can smell her overpowering perfume.

Then she whispered in her cold tone. "Even if you become the Luna, nothing will change the fact that you are a freak! Don't forget who the cursed girl is!!" And then she walks out, leaving Mona terrified and choking with tears.

Tristan saw his mother exits the dining hall, when he reached the room, he saw her in tears. Something inside him welled, as if poked by a sharp object. He approached her but when she saw him, she glared and run off. Now what? He decided to went after his mother.

He found her in her bonsai garden. Somehow, it is her habit. She is pruning a 50-year old miniature oak tree.

"Mom, can we talk?" Tristan spoke as he approched Miranda.

"You are already talking." was her casual response."Please, do me a favor, Mom. Don't be mean to Mona. Soon, she will be my wife and Luna of the pack, she must be treated with respect and dignity. " Tristan asks his mother nicely, the latter still focused on pruning her plant.

"She told you already?" was her cold reply, the snipping sound of her scissors more audible.

"No. I saw you left her in tears." he exhaled, one sign that Tristan is irritated and is trying to keep his cool.

"Maybe she is realizing how unworthy she is for you!" the Luna said forcefully, looking sharply at her son.

"Don't hurt her! Or you'll have to answer me... " Tristan replied, matching his mother's tone.

"Is that a threat, son?"Miranda's brows is in full arch.

"No. Just a reminder." Tristan replied with finality.

"I'll take note of that, but I can't promise much." she said with a vicious smirk on her face as she returned to her bonsai.

Becoming a Black Moon Bride

"Starting today, you will be under my care. Even if I don't like it, I have no choice." Miranda started her lecture to Mona. They are sitting face to face in the huge study room, where the bookshelves rival that of their local library. She looked at Mona's mismatched eyes, those very eyes that gives her the creeps. Mona is just sitting still, maintaining eye contact. Miranda is determined to let Mona understand the extent of her powers as a Luna and that she is standing in the palm of her hands.

"I will teach you everything that I know about the duties and responsibilities of a Luna. You only have to follow what I say. Firstly, a Luna must look good." she said straight. "Have I told you that I don't like you?" she asked her with raising eyebrows.

"You did Luna, a couple of times now." Mona replied quietly, her eye contact is irritating her.

"Great! And it will remain that way. Now, stand up, we will have a trip to Mr. Shaw." she finally ordered Mona as she sashays out of the study.

The Luna is trying to provoke her, Mona thought. But she will not be provoked. She have been into too many tortures and miseries since childhood, and this one is not different. Only a torture in another level. She followed her out of the room, Troy meets her outside the door. He has been in stand-by whenever she's with the Luna and his presence (even if he's just behind the door) it greatly comforts her. As for her fiancee, he's nowhere to be found. He stays more in the Pack House with the Alpha and his father. And whenever he is at home, he makes sure to get out of her way. Great! She sighed. She wishes that she's trained in the Pack House, too. Not because Tristan is there but because of her father. She misses him, and he had not visited her yet nor called her. She's getting worried.

"And you gentleman, you don't need to follow anywhere we go." The Luna speaks behind her regal back.

"Troy." he replied politely.

"What's that?" The Luna abruptly turned to them.

"The name is Troy, Luna. So you wouldn't have to call me gentleman everytime you see me." was Troy's very polite answer.

"I see. Troy. You don't have to come."

"My apologies again Luna, but I have nowhere to go but to follow where Mona will be. That's my duty." he said straightly without any inhibitions.

Miranda's slit of a mouth tightened and her eyes flared. Definitely, she did not like having Troy around.

"Well, suit yourself." she said mockingly. "Let's go." Bruce, her personal assistant appears before her. "Clear all of Mr. Shaw's appointments today. Tell him I will come over." was her command to the PA. The latter immediately nods and made a call. After a minute, Bruce gave the go signal.

Soon, the four of them are on the car heading to some person called Mr. Shaw. Again, great thanks that Troy is with her, she feels secure somehow.

They arrived to a 3-story building with a sign that says Sure Touch. They are in front of the best Beauty Salon in town. The Luna walks in proudly and all employees bow their head and greet her. Talk about a VIP and there is Luna Miranda Jones. They proceed to the third floor and a middle-aged, thin and tall man who looks very handsome and very neat yet odd for Mona greets them. He has a shiny brown head of hair, a very clear glassy skin as if a mannequin and lips in ochre lipstick. He has a vibrant aura in him. A black bar pin with golden writings that says J.Shaw is emblazoned in his blue uniform.

"Luna, what a pleasure. I immediately called my appointments off when I received Bruce's call." his voice is very light, reminding her of sunshine on Summertime.

"Thank you Jim for always accommodating my urgent calls." the Luna said appreciatively.

"So, is she the one?" Mr. Jim Shaw inquired the Luna, already scrutinizing her from head to foot. The Luna just grunted an air of dislike. As always.

"Oh my, my! Such an interesting beauty..." he is moving slowly around her, touching the ends of her hair. "This hair is perfect! And the skin, soft and supple..." he exclaimed, now touching her face lightly. Troy grabbed his hand, an angry look in his face.

"Ooohh, and who are you? Never seen a man as hunky as you..." he touched his chest, his eyes gleaming with excitement and thirst. Confirmed, Jim Shaw is gay. Mona looks at the Luna who is now sitting comfortably in a plush white couch, Bruce standing beside her. Mona also confirms, that the Luna is not happy with Mr. Shaw's reaction to them.

"Jim. Let's go right down to business." The Luna announced irritably.

"Oh sorry Luna. Later, handsome..." he gives Troy a wink before giving his attention to her. He leads her to a seat in front of a large mirror. He touched her hair down to her scalp and started messing it. But her hair is such a real crowning glory, it just goes back straight down to her back.

"Lovely... " he whispered in Mona's ear, definitely impressed by her platinum blonde tresses. He looks at her in the eye and in her face through the mirror. Checking what needs to be changed.

"I don't see any skin problems Luna, and her hair is beyond perfect." Mr. Shaw announced, facing the Luna. Miranda's face is indescribable, her mouth shut even tighter.

"Not perfect yet Jim. Her hair is not natural for someone belonging to the Black Moon pack. It stands out a lot, and we don't like that, do we?" she said hinting sarcasm. "Dye it." she commanded.

Mona looks terrified, maybe her hair makes her stand out in the pack but she loves it. Every inch of it and never in her life would she want to change it. It has become her identity and she don't want anyone to take it away. Even Jim hesistates for a while, his eyeballs moves from her to the Luna.

"But Luna, I thought I'll just have a trim. I don't see any problem with my hair and Mr. Shaw here said it's perfectly fine. " she protested and looked at the Luna still sitting prettily as a queen, checking her painted nails.

"I see you are objecting me, are you Mona?" she speaks so slowly giving her the chills. "My son told me to be nice to you. And here I am just being nice, wanting you to look worthy for him. And yet you are objecting. How shameless of you..." she reiterates slowly, emphasizing each word distastefully. Now she's making Mona look like a shameless, entitled ingrate in front of Jim and Bruce. Troy's features darkened, swallowing his fury. Any more words from the Luna and surely he'll attack.

"Now, if you kindly show some manners, do as I say. Jim! Dye her hair." She commands forcefully. Jim immediately bring Mona to sit again, his eyes wary looking at her through the mirror, her tears stinging her eyes. She glimpse at the Luna, now smirking in victory.

And just like that, after an arduous hair care treatment, her platinum-blonde hair has turned into a rich mud brown. The color the Luna chose-the color that best suits her - the color that will remind her of her righteous place - the mud.

"Now, you look like a real woman from the Black Moon pack. But we still have a problem." She moves behind her and put two small glass canisters in front of her. "Pick one." both of her hands are now on Mona's shoulders

"What is that?!?" Mona asked , her eyes large as saucers.

"See for yourself. Now, pick." she hissed, her hands digging into her collarbone. She gingerly point a finger to the canister in the right.

"Nice choice. Now open it!" the Luna's hands on her shoulders are getting heavier. She take the canister of her choice, she gasped when she saw what's inside. It was a single, amber colored contact lens, the very same color as that of her right eye. "From now on, you will have to wear that contact lens to cover that mismatched eyes of yours. To be honest, it give me the creeps." Her mouth gaping, she glanced at Jim and Troy in the mirror and both are not looking well. "Don't you like my gift, darling?" Miranda said mockingly, squeezing her shoulders tighter, it might leave a bruise later.

"Luna, I can help her put it on. I can teach her how to do it herself too." Jim butt in hesitantly. Mona is heaving her breaths, she is frustrated and angry she wants to cry. But she will not let the Luna see her cry.

"Yeah, sure. Make yourself at home, Jim and make it fast. We still have other appointments for the day." she said and left the room. Bruce followed her.

"Miss Mona, may I..." he interjected and picked the contact lens. He carefully lay it in her left eye as she was facing the ceiling. It stings once it made contact then the sting fades. She blinked a few times to make sure it's properly placed, and it just feels nothing is in there. The mirror reflects not her but she sees another woman in there. Her tears suddenly fell.

"I'm sorry Miss Mona, do you mind if I say something." Jim talks emphatically as he wipes her tears with a Kleenex. She nods as her tears keeps coming.

"I believe you are naturally beautiful. Don't get me wrong but I really am a good judge of character, and the moment you step in I know I like you, that you are rare, the Young Master is very lucky to have you. Don't let the Luna get into your nerves, she's rough and unkind, but it only makes you even better than her. Be strong. Remember that you are still who you are beneath these masks... " he said firmly, looking directly in her eyes. Mona's heart welled with gladness. She never thought that Jim can be as warm and friendly as this.

"Thank you." she said softly, touching his arm and giving it a gentle squeeze.

"Now off you go. The Luna's got a nasty temperament you see. Go on."Troy went to her side and both of them strides to leave.

"And by the way, nice meeting you Mona, and most especially you Mr. Handsome..." he said and winked again to Troy. Troy generously give him a smile, Mona swear she saw Jim heaved a deep breath and left him leaning to a chair for support.

"Now, you look normal." Miranda commented when they were back in the car. The Luna's comment somehow pinched her heart, just because she doesn't look like the rest, she is not normal. But everybody thinks that way about her since childhood. Only her Granny believed and accepted her as she is, plus Troy and lately her Dad. Now, maybe she can add Mr. Shaw on her list. The few people who thinks she is perfect as she is.

They will be visiting the High Priest to have the wedding scheduled. Mona felt giddy upon hearing that they will be going to the Pack House. It only means that she will see her Dad. Everyone in the pack house bows after seeing Miranda. As usual, she is very charismatic and intimidating, no one dares to meet her eyes.

The High Priest is an old,stocky, kind-looking man. According to their books, a priest is chosen by the Moon Goddess herself through a selection ceremony that can last days or months until the goddess had selected the deserving Priest to carry her visions to their kind. How the goddess choose the right man for the task, Mona never knew.

Raymond Sullivan has been the High Priest of the Black Moon Pack for three decades now. And he proves to be a reliable, respected and loyal Pack Priest. He has gray hairs on his balding head and his wrinkles are, well, plentier than his hair.

The Luna and the High Priest have an animated talk together, but whenever he glances her way, he will smile at her kindly. Whenever he talks, she can't help but remember a very kind grandfather whom she never had and never known. Not long, the two agreed upon a date, the wedding will take place two full moons from now. Exactly, two months from now and Mona had never been so nervous.

Claire in the Mirror

"Luna, do we have any more appointments for today?" Mona meek-ly asked Miranda right after they were dismissed by the High Priest.

"Getting tired of my company already Mona-dear?"was Miranda's sweet reply. "Yes. We still have three other appointments. To the clinic, the designer and the wedding planner."

"The clinic?" she asked warily

"You heard me right, the Clinic. To have you checked."

"Me? But I am in good health and--"

"I can see that. But I need to be sure that you don't have any hidden diseases in your body. And of course, to check if your womb is healthy. You'll be carrying my son's children right? I need to be sure that they will come out in this world healthy and NORMAL. Better safe than sorry. " she explained, emphasizing the word NORMAL.

"We still have twenty minutes before Dr. Hans can accommodate us. So, I want to see my husband first. Wait for me in the car." Miranda turned her back to them yet Mona stopped her.

"Luna, can I just go by and see my father quick?" she's hesitant to ask her permission.

"Whatever!" was her only reply and trotted to her husband's office.

"Let's go Troy! Let's find Dad!!" she exclaimed excitedly. Troy nods and smiles at her.

"Where is his office?" Troy asked silently as they climb up the stairs. The Pack house is a massive, six-story brick building. Each floor has designated offices. The Ground Floor holds the huge Hall for Gatherings. It has elevators but they choose the stairs to avoid people coming in and out of the Pack House.

"I don't visit him frequently because he doesn't like to see me before, as you already know. But my Granny did. She oftentimes brings me with her whenever she was asked to come over and deliver things or papers my father had forgotten at home, I just stay out of sight so my Dad won't see me... " she said, smiling wistfully on her memory. "I just hope that they have not change rooms! We are here!" she announced breathlessly. They are on the top floor. The Alpha's floor.They are checking each door signs hoping to find her father's office when they meet the Alpha, William Jones and of course, the Luna. He immediately stopped on his tracks and looked surprised as if he'd seen a ghost.

"Good morning Alpha!" Mona greets him first as she bowed her head.

"Mona?" he asked, surprise is in his tone.

"Yes Alpha. It is me." She said politely. The Alpha glanced at his wife and the Luna just displayed a knowing look.

"I did it. Now she looks like a normal girl of the Black Moon Pack." she said proudly.

"Oh yes. But at first glance I thought you were Claire. With your hair and eyes like that, I thought she came back to life. Good thing it's you. " he said laughing, yet his eyes expressed admiration? The Luna's face on the other hand, looked dimmer as if she had swallowed a bitter pill.

"Let's go, William. Tristan is waiting." she nudged her husband to go.

"If you're looking for Bill, he's not in the office today. He send word that he is sick. But don't worry, he just caught some nasty cold." William assured her. Still Mona is worried.

"Thanks Alpha." was the only words she said. She sighed sadly. Her hopes of seeing her father has gone.

"Do you want me to check on him, Mona?" Troy kindly offered, touching her arm. She looked up at him and smiled. Grateful that she have one loyal friend like him.

"I'd appreciate that Troy." Troy smiled back at her. He is seven years older than her and was a rogue before he was imprinted to her. Now he stands as her personal body guard especially that the Luna is a constant threat to her. He is strong and muscular, handsome in his own way and has a beautiful tan complexion. Troy exudes an aura of danger when angry, and warmth in normal days. She likes Troy because he cares for her a lot, stands between her and to anyone who wishes to harm her, and her greatest comforter since Josephine had died. He is ruggedly handsome with a scar on his cheek that only adds to his appeal. His black hair is shiny and thick, and his dark eyes holds a thousand secrets. His chest is hard like concrete, and Mona feels secure everytime she is in his embrace. So she did, embraced Troy.

"What is this for?" he asked looking abashed, Troy the man of steel was caught off-guard.

"My advance thank you for checking out Dad." she said sweetly.

"Alright, you don't have to do that." he said pulling away laughing. He messed the top of her head. "You're such a kid." he said as he messed her hair even more. Mona laughed and let him just mess her hair.

Tristan was on the hallway now, thinking about his loads of paperwork waiting on his table. Then he saw a very familiar figure. He's positive that it is Troy, hugging a girl who looks very familiar too. And when he pulled back, she looks at him with those happy eyes, something within Tristan explodes.Tristan clenched his fist on what he saw. Mona, his fiancee is flirting with her body guard. He really don't feel good with that Troy guy hanging around Mona, and his instincts are always correct. Mona on the other hand, seems to be enjoying his company. Seriously, what is going on between them? He feels that the hot boiling sensation with in him has risen, he would like to punch him in the face once and for all. A voice stops him.

"Tristan, your mother wants me to give you this." a sweet voice echoed in the hall. It was Leizel handing out a brown envelope to him. Once more, his heart did a backflip. Leizel's effects on him is as strong as before, she could still make him go out of his senses. Suddenly his anger was extinguished. Mona looked to them and he made sure that she will see how he touched Leizel's hand. But it is undeniable that he still have overflowing feelings for Leizel. He want to curse her for what she did but his heart had forgiven her already. He have almost killed Henry upon knowing his betrayal. He was his bestfriend yet he never told him anything. He just let him fall for her too deep before he learned about their relationship and vow leaving him devastated.

"Thank you Leiz. Maybe you can help me sort some folders in the office."he replied huskily.

"Tristan, please..."she whispered pleading, mostly restraining her emotions. Their bond maybe broken but there still has remnants of emotions in her heart.

"Yes, you will help me." he finally said and took her hand on his. Leizel just followed. They walked towards Troy and Mona, and he smirked in her face.

Once Tristan and Leizel passed by them, Mona and Troy just exchanged looks.

"You fine?" Troy said, worry is in his voice.

"Of course! Why shouldn't I?" she shrugged. But deep inside, there is a little pinch in her heart. Troy looks at her in disbelief, his eyebrow rising.

"Trust me. I am more attached to you than to him!" she laughs and led him to the elevator. "Let's use the elevator now, the stairs are tiring." Troy just smiled at her.

After the general check up in the Clinic where Dr. Hans concluded that Mona is in excellent condition with a healthy womb at top of that, Miranda looks more grim. Maybe the Luna is hoping that she may have health issues to raise her claim that she is not fitting to be an Alpha's bride. Well, sorry not sorry. Thanks to her Granny's 18 years of tender loving care, her health and body is perfect.

They proceed to the designer to pick her wedding gown. And according to the Black Moon tradition, the bride will wear a gown in midnight blue, as they believed, it is the Moon Goddess' color. As usual, Miranda picked the gown for her. She picked a midnight blue trumpet gown in satin and lace material. It hugs her body perfectly, her figure fully emphasized. It has a low back design exposing her creamy skin. Ms. Joyce, the designer never stop her compliments and admiration. Mumbling how pretty Mona is.

Ms. Joyce is pretty herself. She's like a supermodel, very tall and she has slight similarities with Gigi Hadid. Her entire aura shouts elegance and sophistication. She's wearing a peach coat and slacks, white silky inner, and minimal jewelries. Her shoulder-length straight light brown hair is tied in a pony tail. She's wearing a make up that greatly accentuates her lovely cheekbones. Mona estimates her to be as old as Troy. She is now adjusting the zipper of her dress as she face herself in the mirror. Mona still can't believe that the reflection on the mirror is her. She's her but isn't. She lost deep in her thoughts until Ms. Joyce speaks, her voice musical.

"You look like your mother. The similarities are uncanny as if I am seeing her alive and well."

"You know my Mom?" she looked startled

"Of course! Who would not know her. She is the most beautiful woman in the pack. " She smiled as if reminiscing a beautiful memory.

"She and my Mom are bestfriends. I was four years old when she was at this same spot. Fitting a gown for her wedding. She was exquisite... My mom was her designer and is already running this shop. It was just a tiny shop before but as you can see, we have expanded. "

"I have not met my Mom." sadness in her voice, now she can place where she'd seen the woman in the mirror who looks just like her but isn't. Her Mom's huge portait in her father's study. Her eyes swim with tears. "I don't have any memory of her either. She died early after my birth."

"Yeah. That's very sad. My mom was devastated too. She was an amazing woman, both beautiful in heart and soul."

"I wish I met her." she whispered.
"You are already meeting her." Joyce gently squeezes her shoulder.

"Claire?!?" a surprised and unbelieving voice speaks behind them. Both at them looked at the mirror and saw an elegant-looking woman in her fifties or so.

"Mom!" Joyce exclaimed. "I was just talking about you and here you are!" She said happily and hugged her mother. Mona faced them, she felt a little jealousy looking at them, seeing how sweet and lovely their bond is. Could they be like them too, if her mother had lived? She smiled sadly.

"I thought I was seeing Claire back to life. I couldn't believe my eyes." Joyce's mom is teary eyed.

"Mom, this is Mona Mayfield. She's your best friend Claire's daughter. Mona, this is my Mom, Joeylyn Wilson"

"Hello dear! I am glad to see you." Mrs. Wilson hugged her and give her wet kisses on both of her cheeks. She's crying, muttering how she misses Mona's mother.

"Mom, you're making Mona uncomfortable." Joyce speaks to her mother. "She's our client."

"Oh sorry. I couldn't help myself. Pardon my rudeness..." Mrs.. Wilson replied in a low tone.

"It's okay Mom. I understand..." Mona said politely.

Joeylyn touched Mona's face and smiled sadly. Mona knows that she's seeing her mother in her.

"The last time I saw her was when she was fitting her wedding dress. She was soo beautiful..." Mrs. Wilson started, her fingers moving to the silky satin of her gown.

"Yes. I bet she was beautiful and was totally perfect for my father." Mona uttered silently.

"But it was not your father whom she'll marry though.. " Mrs. Wilson said in a hushed voice. Mona looked suprised. If her mother was not going to marry her father, then who? As if Mrs. Wilson was able to read her mind, she replied.

"She's about to marry William Jones. The Alpha."

Under Claire's Shadows

The Luna entered the room irritably, she let Mona twirl for her and gives her a very hesistant OK. Mona still has questions about her mother and her intriguing love affair with the Alpha. But the Luna's temper changed from nice to gruesome as soon as Mrs. Wilson mentions her mother's name and their resemblance and on how beautiful she is. She bade goodbye to the mother and daughter, wherein the latter gives her a calling card (not the business one) that has her personal contact number, home number and home address. Mrs. Wilson invites her for tea whenever she's free. She put the calling card on her pocket and made a mental note to place it among her important keepsakes.

The Luna on the other hand, cancels the appointment with the wedding planner, saying she's done for the day. For Mona, that is a good thing. She's tired of her snide remarks too.

She immediately went to her room and lay there thinking how she crave for her mom's presence. How little she knew about her and her many what ifs. She took the calling card in her pocket and stared at it for a long time. A knock wakes her from her reverie.

"Can I come in?" It was Troy. She immediately stood up and ran to the door.

"Hi! How's Dad?" it was her excited greeting.

"Getting better. But his cold is really nasty." he reported

"Did he went to the clinic for a check up? What about medicine? Is he eating well?" these are Mona's tirade of questions, Troy just backs off giggling.

"He'll be fine Mona. Your Dad is strong, a cold won't take him down. Don't stress yourself too much. And when he's up and going, he promised to visit you." Troy said reassuring her.

"Really? But I can stop myself from worrying. I'd still want you to check on him once in a while to make sure he's fine... " she said stubbornly.

"Yes, I will. What's that? " pointing to the calling card in her hand.

"Mrs. Wilson's calling card. She's my Mom's bestfriend and she invited me for tea. She is very nice. I like her." she told him animatedly including her meeting with the gorgeous designer Ms. Joyce. Mona thinks that Joyce and Troy will be a perfect match! She laughs about it.

"What's funny?" he asked, a brow arching.

"Nothing!" she giggled as a child. Maybe she'll introduce him to Ms. Joyce and see what will happen. She giggle even more.

"What is it?" Troy asked raising his voice a pitch higher. He don't like it when Mona is acting like that, she's surely making something in her head that undoubtedly includes him.

"Nothing, okay? I am just thinking for a long bubble bath." she said still smiling sheepishly. Troy just rolled his eyes on her. How many times would he tell her that she's not a good liar? She immediately run to her bathroom laughing. Troy left Mona's room and decided to take a walk.

Mona forgot what time it was, guess she enjoyed her time in the bath. She went out and covered herself with a bathrobe. Her hair dripping wet, she wrapped a towel to it. She immediately went to the walk-in closet but shrugs and left, realizing those are not her clothes. Wait. What? She opened it again and it really was not her clothes! All there in were branded dresses and apparels. Her sneakers were gone too, and were replaced with sandals in varying heels' height. She gaped. A maidservant was arranging her covers, she asked went to the gi amd asked hysterically.

"Where are my clothes?" she turned to the maidservant. The latter looked down, guilty eh?

"The Luna ordered us to remove all your clothes and replace it with those." she politely replied

"What?!? But those are my belongings! Where is it?" she yelled, unbelieving that they violated her personal space.

"She made us throw them- your clothes Miss. We throw them as ordered by the Luna..." she answered silently, fear is hinted in her voice.

Mona gaped, unbelieving, shaking her head briskly, the towel on her head fell down. "This is what you will do. Bring back all my belongings!! All of them! Right now!" her voice thunders across her room, the girl was startled.

"Yes, miss." she hurriedly went out of the door. Mona slumped down on her bed, staring at the exposed walk in closet and the clothes there in. She's exasperated. A moment later, the Luna walked in her room.

"Well, well, well. I see you don't like my gifts." Miranda slowly utter each word as she entered her room. "I was expecting a thank you for my efforts to make you look deserving but you keep on restraining all of it! You are really very ungrateful!" she said in gritted teeth.

"But at least you should tell me. Those are my things, and some of them holds sentimental value. You cannot rip it away from me like that. I am not refusing all you want to give me, but it wouldn't hurt I guess to alert me first on what you will do...." Mona was speaking fast, hurt and anger in her every word.

"I want to make it clear to you, Mona Mayfield. You will not tell me what to do. I will do what I want, and you will follow ALL OF IT! If I tell you to stay, you will STAY. And if I tell you to jump, you will JUMP! Am I clear?!?" the Luna's voice is thundering in her room, scaring her wits out. The Luna never fails to intimidate her with her dominance and presence.

"I understand Luna. But please, let me have my belongings. At least, Troy can send them back home." she pleads, her eyes shut.

"Making your bargain eh?" she said sarcastically.

"Mona, what's the problem?!" Troy burst in her room, he looked grimly at the Luna.

"Well, you do as you wish. But I don't like to see you wearing your filthy rags again!" she looked meanly to both of them before she leave, slamming the door behind her.

Miranda is pissed. Really pissed off with Mona. Even when the girl has not said anything or even if she's still, her presence angers her. Especially now that she is actually seeing what people are seeing in her. It was a reckless move of her to have Mona's hair dyed, she thought it will add pain to Mona (which she saw in the salon and pleased her) but now she wished she did not have it done. She is seeing again the face of the woman she hated since she became William's mate. The only woman who made her feel inferior. The woman who stole the affection of her mate! Claire died eighteen years ago, yet she made it possible for the people who loves Claire to see her again through her daughter Mona. How dumb was she not to see their similarities, and a fool not to use her forethought. Now, she have to swallow this pill she'd made. "I am alive and well. And you are dead. You cannot take away my man. I have your daughter , I will see to it that she will be miserable as long as I live!" Miranda whispered in the ebbing night.

Troy had not returned since he brought her things home. She picked few of her beloved clothes and hid it well in case of emergency. She has been wearing the clothes the Luna had provided and as much as she hate it, she can't do anything. She's always wearing dresses not longer than her knees and shoes not lower than two inches. Her feet has never been tired wearing it. She had been into various lessons already including etiquettes, manners, make up, politics, memorizing the pack clans all over the land and etcetera, Mona swears her head will burst anytime. The Luna is always there, observing, correcting, lecturing, insulting her. Somehow, Mona is starting to be immune to her harsh words, just like what she did everytime her peers bully her.

"Tomorrow, we will attend a meeting with the other Lunas from other packs. It is time that you will be introduced to them, it is a very important gathering because you will get to know all the women behind the powerful alphas from all over the land." she finally announced.

"Yes Luna." was her only reply

"Be proper and presentable. Show your manners. I am afraid of the stupid things you'll do in there.It is a gathering of women with class and thorough breeding, behave yourself or else, you'll be excluded. My son won't like it if his bride causes troubles .." the Luna reiterates, smirking every once in a while.

"No Luna. I will act accordingly." she swear, looking straight to the Luna's eyes.

"Good." Miranda respond before she left her in the study.

They left the town early, the congregation of Lunas will be held in one of the five star hotels in the city. The Luna made it a point to let her wear a glittering long dress in pale pink. She can't help but think she looks like a disco ball. Her straight hair was styled in waves that reminds her that of mermaids and glistening hairpins adorn her hair. The Luna looks sharp and intimidating, yet elegant as always.

The hall was filled when they arrived. Lunas from other packs stood from each other as if sizing up who has the best outfit. Mona feels like the congregation is somehow a gathering of beauty queens. All were wearing classy and flashy clothes, even the oldest Luna whom she thinks to be in her 60's, made sure that she's still stunning. There are twenty Luna's in all, from the greatest to the lesser packs. The head of all packs is the Blue Moon Pack, and is represented by Grand Luna Narcissa Holmes. The 60 year-old Luna in her stunning black dress. Mona also observes that every pack has a distinct hair color, for instance the Golden Moon Pack where the Luna has shiny golden hair, Scarlet Moon Pack Luna with her bright red hair (if she remembers right, Luna Miranda belongs in this pack too), the Grey Moon Pack (ashen colored hair) and their pack, The Black Moon (with brown to black hair except her of course, she's got naturally platinum blonde hair whom the Luna dyed to mud brown). None of the packs present have the same natural hair color as hers which made Mona thinks that she really is different.

The gathering began, they were seated in a long table with ice sculpture centerpieces in the shapes of wolves adorning it. Foods were served by course as the women gave updates from their packs. New Lunas and Lunas- to-be were introduced and that includes her. Everyone seems to be pleasant and good-natured except Miranda, who is waiting for her to make mistakes. Somehow, she was able to meet them all and lucky enough make few friends.

"I am pleased to meet you Mona of the Black Moon pack. I hope that we can be of help to you when your time comes." Narcissa pleasantly said to her.

"Thank you Grand Luna Narcissa. I am honored of your acceptance." Mona replied politely.

"Pardon me, but upon looking at you, you remind me of a very nice girl who was presented in this very venue a long ago. Claire Thorne was her name. She looks exactly just like you... " Narcissa said smiling at her. Miranda's face dimmed.

"Maybe you mean my mother. She was Claire Thorne, and became Claire Mayfield when she married my father..." Mona answered politely.

"Yes and so I heard about her sad fate, she really was sweet and a beautiful soul. Such a loss!" Luna Narcissa added, glancing at Miranda once in a while. The other women who knew her Mother also shared bits of stories and sane sentiments about her mother. It thrilled Mona, these women telling stories about how lovely a woman her mother was. Now her longing to the mother she never met intensified.

"You know, she was even hailed the Wolf Queen before. It was a beauty contest represented by chosen women from all packs during the Carnival Season. And there she was, winning the crown effortlessly, though I can say that she really deserved it. She's got beauty, brains, and power. Her wolf was stunning as well! By the way, I just came second to her.. " The Golden Moon Luna, Jessica Mills started her story, she's smiling and laughing at her own memory. The other women laughs too. Someone cleared her throat.

"Well my dear Lunas, maybe we can let the dead rest, should we? We still have lots of issues to discuss... " Miranda spoke. There was a sudden silence and the clamor began once more.

Miranda is unhappy with the event. She was hoping to put Mona in the dirt in front of those women but the heck of them, making her a fool! Scrubbing salt in her scars, relieving stories about her and pleasing that girl of an idiot-Mona! Miranda's bitter resentment to Claire Thorne-Mayfield grows bigger. Now she's gritting her teeth in anger and resentment to the girl in front of her who bears Claire's face.

"You seemed pleased... " Miranda spoke sarcastically. They are now in the car, going back to their pack.

"Yes Luna. I never heard much about my mother, I never thought they knew her. It was fun knowing that my Mom was quite popular during her days. Also, I learned so much from them. I'm glad you brought me in the gathering. Thank you Luna." Mona answered gratefully. Miranda on the other hand just clenched her fists.

Remnants of a Broken Bond

M ona has been improving in all of her lessons, somehow she had adjusted to the daily tasks given by the Luna, being immune to her insults helps her best. The preparations for the wedding are on the process with only two weeks before the day. Still, Mona has thoughts whether she'll make a fine wife or not. Perhaps, she just don't feel like marrying yet, at the same time, afraid to taint her father's reputation and be removed from the pack. Mona didn't have fabulous choices either so she must do the best of it. Thalia, her wolf, has not surfaced since the rogues attacked, she's wondering what has happened to her. She can't take her wolf form too no matter how hard she tried. She hadn't spoken to her since Tristan chose her as his bride. Has she turned dormant? If that is so, it will be a big trouble. Especially if the Luna learns about it, surely, she'll do anything to disclaim her.

The Luna arranged a meeting with the women's circle. A Luna must have a council of her own, it is composed of five very eligible ladies from the pack (she can include her lady friends if she have, but in her case, the Luna handpicked ladies of her choice.) To her disgust, Paula and Myrtle (her avid bullies) were members of the circle. Leizel James has a seat too, which of course is making her so uncomfortable, a very rich and sophisticated yet bratty girl named Daniella Rodriguez and to her relief, Joyce Wilson (the only girl she can trust among others). Paula, Myrtle and Daniella sure are conniving with the Luna to carry out her plans to destroy and give her more sufferings. Just great. Get it on, baby!

She arrived in the hall, the ladies are all seated in the long table. The Circle's purpose is to give counsel, reports, updates and carry out the Luna's plans and projects for the pack. Also, as women they will serve as the ambassadors, at the same time, the backbone of the Pack, to support and help in the Alpha's decisions and visions. Above all, to maintain the balance in the pack. They will be the Luna's ally, adviser,and friend in times of troubles. Mona just laughs at the idea that Paula and Myrtle will be her friends, the way they look at her is enough to swallow her whole.

"Good morning Ladies! I called you today to announce that starting today, you are officially a member of the Luna's Circle." Miranda announced to the girls, a maidservant giving out booklets to the ladies.

"Read the booklet, written therein are your roles and duties to your Luna and your pack. You must oblige to all of your Luna's commands and help her. This time, you are more than just council members, but sisters." Paula smirked at the Luna's last words.

"You are expected to be trustworthy, honest, and loyal to your Luna. Any-one who will betray her trust means exclusion from the pack." Miranda continued.

"Now ladies, swear your loyalty to your Luna."

The ladies placed their hand in their chest and all at once pronounced their loyalty creed.

"Thank you, Ladies. In a few weeks, Mona here will become the new Luna of the Black Moon Pack. You must treat her with respect and speak with her in all honesty and fairness." Mona heard Miranda's words right but it seems to be oozing with sarcasm, her ears hurt. After that, she left them to have time for themselves.

"I am glad that I am part of your council Miss Mona, I promise you can count on me." Joyce assured her, the three other girls just smirked.

"Yeah, whatever... " Daniella said prickly. She looks like a Mexican actress with her olive skin and curly black hair, she's wearing a very red lipstick and false eyelashes. She find her pretty even without those make up but her attitude problem is overpowering her entire physique. "I need to go. I still have a date." she said uninterestingly. "And for you future Luna, good luck." and off she glided out the door. Myrtle and Paula laughs heartily.

"I just want to make it clear to you Mona... Maybe Young Master Tristan chose you as his bride and Luna, but you. You will remain as the freak of the pack. Don't feel so high and mighty of yourself." it was Paula in her bitchy tone.

"How dare you! You swore a moment ago to serve the Luna with respect and protect her with all your life, how dare you say those words to her! " Joyce stood up, looking angry at Paula and Myrtle.

"I did swore but it so happened that I am not referring to her as my Luna. Only Luna Miranda is the Luna I will bow my head with!" Paula hissed

"Come on, Joyce. Don't be a prick! You should choose your friends wisely, you know. Paula's family is rich and powerful, and we love your designs and clothes, we don't want it closed, don't we?" Myrtle chimed in.

"Are you threatening me?" Joyce suddenly looked fierce.

"Oh no. No, Miss Joyce. I am not. I am just... reminding." Myrtle added sweetly. "And we also have here the ever charming Leizel James. How does it feel like to be the woman torn between two lovers??" she turned to Leizel, the other girl tensed up. "Luna Miranda, as I may say is very wise indeed in choosing the Luna's Circle. I say you will be challenged during your term." Paula remarked snidely to Mona.

She tapped the table and stood, moving closer to both Paula and Myrtle. She is done with their attitudes, she won't let them disrespect her again. She smirked at them as she said her words slowly, letting them feel the weight of her every word.

"Guess what? You maybe rich, powerful, beautiful but it will stop there. I will be Luna, and you will be nothing but my subjects. The Luna's words still has more power than your mere existence so know your place! Don't dare threaten me again nor humiliate me or else... your pretty heads will be such a waste... " Mona speaks fiercely to Myrtle and Paula, intimidating them. She never had that courage before, and the feeling is exhilarating. Paula and Myrtle backed down, frightened by Mona's new-found fire. "Understood?"

"Yes, Miss Mona." they said retreating, Paula in her defiant face. Somehow, she finally gave Paula a notion not to take her easily.

"Good. To that, I have no business to both of you. Leave!" she said harshly the two ladies hurriedly went out the hall.

"Serves them right!" Leizel chirped. "I never liked Paula and Myrtle too. They were brats and so entitled."

She gave Leizel a warm smile. Maybe she can get along with her. Mona couldn't believe that she did what she just did. Joyce tapped her shoulders, reassuring that she did a very fine job shutting Paula and Myrtle.

"By the way, I have to go. I still have lots of clients today. Call me if you need anything." Joyce told Mona as she hurriedly went out the door. She was waving her goodbye at the door when Troy came in. The two almost collided if only Troy is not agile to step away on Joyce's way. Well, there was an instant connection between the two making Mona's inner self rejoice.Joyce went out flushed.

"You need anything Troy?" Mona inquired, Troy was still looking for the woman who just left. He saw Mona's mischievous smile playing on her lips. He cleared his throat.

"Nothing. I was just checking." he formally said, avoiding Mona's eyes. He can see her teasing look and she won't stop bugging him after this.

"Leiz, you never told me that you will be here. " Tristan spoke from behind. Leizel tensed up again.

Mona looked at the two old lovers. "Come, Troy. I need to tell you something. Goodbye Leizel! See you around! " she said cheerfully to Leizel then she grabbed Troy away from the room leaving Tristan and Leizel behind. The latter went out of the room and started going to the drive way. She hushed Troy and follow them there.

"Leizel, are you avoiding me?" Tristan asked almost pleading. Leizel shrugs her shoulders. "Tell me, Leiz... "

"Tristan, please. Stop it okay? I don't want trouble. I'm happy now... " Leizel said firmly.

"Are you?" Tristan retorted "Why does it feel like you're not?"

"Pull yourself together Tristan! You are about to be married in two weeks and you're not being reasonable!!" she hushed him irritably.

"This is just the remnants of the bond, don't confuse it with your emotions. We are done!" she said with conviction.

"It will be unfair to Mona if you keep on looking out for another woman. Please Tristan... I don't want to be trapped in our broken bond, I am doing all I can to fight it. I hope you do the same ... " Leizel speaks in his face. Tristan clenched his fists, unwilling to accept her words.

"Mona? Is that you?" another voice speaks up. Mona looked up at the source of the voice.

"Hi! What are you two doing here?" It was Henry. Upon seeing Henry's eyes, something within Mona moved, and her heart suddenly welled with affection and longing and pain? She can't understand what she's feeling, to be honest. Her heart seemed to beat slowly. Troy grabbed her arm as he faced Henry, wary and alarmed. Tristan and Leizel looked their way. Of course, they just spoiled their moment.

Tristan looked at Henry angrily and his anger doubled upon seeing how he looks at Mona. His jaw tightened and his face darkened.

Henry had not seen Mona after Tristan's party. A part of his heart was wallowing because of breaking his bond to Mona, somehow he regretted it. She made his heartbeat stopped that night and swore he was an idiot. Looking at her now, she is even more beautiful with his dark hair and amber eyes. He saw her lately in town, looking good and fine and he thought he'll be fine too. But he was wrong. Emotions started to stir within him. He is also pissed with this Troy guy who never leaves Mona's side. Pissed and jealous at the same time. And there was Tristan, with a furious look in his face. Is he mad because he is looking at Mona or because Leizel chose him? But Mona's pull is much stronger, he can't take his eyes off her.

"Leave her alone. " Troy said with a threatening look. Mona seemed to wake from her trance.

"Stop Troy! Let's go." She grabbed his arm and turned away from them. He can feel the chilly aura sorrounding the three men. The least she wanted was have Troy fight with them. She wants Henry that's for sure.

But she won't let the remnants of the bond overpower her. She left Henry with difficulty, she felt her heart crushing. She thought she was over him, she thought she had forgotten about him since that unfateful night. But it actually never went away.

"I would like to punch him in the face for once, Mona." Troy broke her silence. They are in the hallway now, away from them.

"Don't do that. I don't want you getting hurt over useless reasons." She said to him, as she fell out of balance, Troy caught her. The encounter has taken her energy, she shut her eyes and calm herself.

"You okay?" Troy asked worriedly.

"Yes. No.. I am just...let me just stay this way." she is at loss for words, she leaned to Troy's chest as she gave herself a silent cry. A cry she don't know the reason. Maybe her heart just want to cry? She gave in.

Tristan is furious. But Leizel stopped him from doing something stupid. They left before he can even say a word. He went back to the manor and saw Mona as she tripped and Troy caught her. His jaw tightened and he clenched his fist. How dare him to touch his bride! He was moving closer to them but he stopped on his tracks when he heard her little sobs. Somehow, pain struck him. He forgot that Henry had rejected her for Leizel and she must feel it too. The remnants of a broken bond. In fact, they are on the same boat. Still hurting whenever the person who rejected them shows up. Getting irrational in their presence. How long will it be until he can fight it off? How long will she able to bear the pain?

Suddenly, Tristan felt silly and helpless. Why did he blurted out her name during the party? Why was she so beautiful that night, in the first place, making him forget his pain from the rejection, capturing his attention all night? Also, why is he acting like an idiot adding to her misery? And why on earth, he feels jealous with Troy as he leisurely touches her hair as she cry on his shoulders? Above all, Tristan can't fathom why he feels sad seeing Mona in tears. He touched his chest and felt his heart beating out of rhythm.

One Rhythm

The following days was filled with their tiring appearances on public. Tristan and Mona went to places together, meeting important people, establishing themselves as a couple, officially accepting one another as soon to be husband and wife. If they were ordinary people who happened to be in love with each other or for a more fitting description, that they are together through the mate bond, they could have been enjoying these moments and appearances together. Since, they are neither from the options given nor friends for starters, they seemed to be walking on eggshells. Uncomfortable, unfamiliar, unreal. These are Mona's feelings right now. After meeting the Alpha's council, she really had enough. The suffocating attention given to them, their fake affection to each other just to please these people, her confused heartbeats in his nearness. Mona sighed.

Tristan is feeling odd as well. His heart is beating crazily, he is trying his hardest to be calm and firm. They just finished meeting his council and he thought he looks dumb and pretentious. Yes, Mona is a very fitting pair for him, the council likes her wit too. But there is no denying that love is absent and pretending has become the name of the game. He can feel it too, Mona is uncomfortable with him. Thanks goodness, the meeting is over. They are now in the car, going back to the Manor. He's driving, she is looking out in the window, silence has never been this loud before. Glancing at her, he can't help but admire her simplicity.

She suddenly looked at him and Tristan thought he swallowed his tongue the moment their eyes made contact. He returned his gaze in the road.

"I know a place just beyond that woods. It's pretty. Would you like to see it, breath some fresh air like that?" Tristan blurted out of the blue. He scold himself for it.

"Is it really nice?" Mona replied, her voice tired.

"Why don't you see for yourself so you could be the better judge." he smiled loosing his tensed nerves.

"Okay." was her only reply. Tristan parked the car beside the road and they hop out of it. They walked down the path to the woods, feeling the breeze on their skin.

This is what Mona needs. A little walk on the woods. It seems forever since she last took a walk in the woods and it feels great. Her tension is starting to disappear. Her eyes now is combing through the trees and vegetation, she missed this. She stopped in her tracks and spread her arms, closed her eyes and inhaled the scent of the woods.

Tristan smiled looking at her, appreciating the view in front of him. Mona is wearing a powder blue sun dress just below her knees, she topped her dress with a blazer for a more conventional look, her straight hair flowing freely in her back, the look in her eyes and the very simple way she smiles. His heart flutters in a beautiful way. He remembered the eight-year old Mona during the camp. Pretending to have a stomach ache after her team mates bullied her, running to the woods and stopping by the majestic falls. He was there when she was silently sketching in her sketchpad, happy and contented on where she was, away from the boys and girls who does nothing but make fun of her. Right then, his young self had known that he would like to protect her no matter what happened.

"Tristan? Are you okay?" Mona wake him in his thoughts. He had not noticed, he'd been staring at her for a while.

"This way..." he leads the way. "I used to go here when I want to be alone. When I need some me-time."

"Wait. This means this is your personal place, are you sure you want to show it to me?" Mona asked, hesitating to step some more.

"Yeah. Positive." he smiled at her. "You will appreciate it more than I do. Come." he held his hand to her, Mona reached for it. The moment her hand touched his, Tristan knew he needs to uphold the promise he made himself ten years ago, behind the tree while looking at then eight-year old Mona who was happily sketching on her pad, that he, Tristan Jones, will protect her with all his life. And evident as well was a little unknown emotion that has started to bloom in the corner of his heart.

They reached the clearing and it is indeed beautiful. The clearing looks like a sea of flowers. The wind blows mildly with a relaxing and sweet fragrance. Butterflies are everywhere, birds on the trees are singing in harmony. It makes their senses at work. Tristan knew she'll love it and he's satisfied seeing the look on her face. Mona stares at the clearing for a long time, taking it all in.

"So beautiful... " she whispered softly. Her heart is welling with so much joy, she remembered her Granny and her love for flowers, the flower garden back in her home, her quiet time in the falls, everything. She had not noticed she already has tears in her face.

"It's beautiful here!" she exclaimed, smiling and wiping her tears at the same time. Tristan gathered a bunch of flowers and moved closer to Mona.

Everything seemed to stay still. Even the birds stopped singing and the wind stopped blowing.

Tristan is moving to her slowly, flowers in his hand, a beautiful smile on his face, and her heart singing a song she never heard before.

"For you... " she heard him, his voice deep and he is very close. She accepted the flowers and smelled them. They smelled so sweet. As she looked up, she saw his eyes full of words he can't say and passion he never thought he have. Mona closed her eyes and the last thing she knew, Tristan's warm lips was on hers. The kiss was sweet and serene, his hand on his waist was light and warm. As he kissed her deeper, she cling on his neck, taking everything all in. The rush of beautiful emotions was raining on both of them. He leaned on her forehead, still with his eyes closed. Not wanting the magical moment to end, listening to the music of their heartbeats, humming the same rhythm.

"Mona!! What a surprise, we have been talking about you and here you are!" Mrs. Joey Lyn Wilson greets her cheerfully. Encasing her in a warm hug. "Come! Come!" Mrs. Wilson invited her inside her home. She had been meaning to visit her, but because of her busy schedule, she wasn't able to make it until today. Tristan dropped her off to the Wilson's home after they went to the clearing. What happened there was magical and she can feel her face blushing.

"How are you, dear? I understand that you are very busy. Thanks goodnesss that you were able to squeeze me in your busy schedule." she said, leading her to the sitting room. She asked her maid to bring them tea and brownies.

"We're not so busy today. So I thought I'll visit you now."

"Great! Just great! How did you find our house? I hope the neighborhood did not confuse you..." Mrs. Wilson said as she laughed.

"Not really.. Actually, Tristan drive me here. He knows the neighborhood too well." Mona answered.

"Oh yes. Such a sweet kid." she commented. Upon mentioning him, her face blushed again. Thankfully, the other woman did not notice. "I am glad that you will be marrying Tristan. I knew him well, he is kind and gentle and caring and responsible. Well, he will be a fine husband for you. Just like his father." she smiled while holding both her hands.

"You mentioned before that my Mom was engaged to the Alpha before... How did it happen?" she said, her curiosity getting the best of her.

"Well, it happened a long, long time ago. You see, we were childhood friends, the three of us. William, Claire and I. We grew up in this very same neighborhood. Playing all day under the sun, attending the same school, and playing some more." Mrs. Wilson started as she went to the nearby bookshelf and took a dusty photo album. She handed it to her. She started leafing through the pages of the album and seemed to be taken back in time.

"William's parents were very kind and loving, they've given him the freedom to play among us, common pack kids." Mona looked through the photo album and saw photos of their younger selves. Her Mom was pretty at her age, always wearing a bright smile and her eyes were always full of happiness. She looks very carefree. Young Mrs. Wilson was a shy type, she looks timid in almost all of her photos. The young Alpha looks mischievous and playful. He can see young Tristan in him. They seemed to have a happy childhood, very far from hers.

"Everyone knew they were an item. A lovely couple they will be. They represented the essence of the Black Moon pack. Beauty and Strength. Grace and Power. Wisdom and Mercy.. " Mrs. Wilson said dreamily. "But those days were unlike today where rules were followed strictly. And loving outside the mate-bond was prohibited. Whoever the person fated to you by the Moon Goddess will be the one and no one can defy it. At sixteen, their mates have not yet appeared, whereas, we all have found our rightful mates. We thought that the Moon Goddess was finally giving them a chance to be together. I was very happy for them as their friend. Of course." she smiled wearily. Mona just listened silently.

"At twenty, their mates have not shown up yet. And so, they decided to take their relationship to the next level. William proposed to Claire and she accepted. All the preparations were made and I even designed and made her wedding gown in my very own shop, I can see Claire's beaming face. She was divine." Mrs. Wilson is so immersed in her story, she seemed to be transported back in time. "Right there, I knew they were made for each other."

"But I was wrong. Two weeks before the wedding, the old Alpha and William went to the Scarlet Moon Pack to pay their respect to the funeral of the late Alpha Luke, the Alpha of the said pack. And there he met Miranda. His mate. The mate chosen by the Moon Goddess for him." she retold these sadly. " William and Claire's wedding was off. He returned with a new bride. Claire was devastated but she knew this will happen one day. You must understand that the mate bond must be followed. Prior arrangements and relationships must be ended, erased, and forgotten." her tone was even sadder.

"What happened to my Mom after?" she inquired looking at the old womans face.

"She was a remarkable woman. She accepted it without any hesitation. You see, both of them were so in love with each other, yet they have no power against the mate bond. They accepted their fate whole heartedly. But I know, they both reserved each other special places in their hearts." she smiled wistfully.

"And my father? How did he met my father?" Mona asked again

"Bill is William's bestfriend. But he was studying in Europe that time, the reason Claire and him had never met. Bill only went home for his wedding, He was William's best man. I know, Claire was still hurt by the recent changes, yet everyone was expected in the wedding. No one should miss it. And there, your father and mother met."

"He was a good man, your father. And Claire learned to loved him in no time especially the power of the mate bond overwhelming them. And they lived happily together." Mona was somehow happy about the turn of events, and glad that her Mom was able to love again despite their devastating break up.

"I never thought that my Mom has almost became the Luna of the pack. That was really unexpected. I really have a lot to know about my Mom." Mona said quietly.

"You don't have to be sad about it Mona. Surely, your mom has been with you all through your life. She has never actually left you. She stays in your heart." Mrs. Wilson hugged her, gently tapping her back.

"I know." she hugged her back. Mrs. Wilson wiped the mist in her glasses with a handkerchief, she remained silent for a while. As if lost in thought.

"What are you thinking about Mrs. Wilson?" she asked the woman as she sipped her tea.

Mrs. Wilson only left her with an enigmatic remark. "I was thinking that some great love never really dies. It lives and keeps you alive. It even transcends through time. Remember that. "

Mona was confused with it, although she just gave Mrs. Wilson a nod of contentment as she bid her goodbye.

Miranda's Wrath

"Mona! Hello!" William greets Mona as he came across the girl in the garden. He is smoking his pipe and is enjoying a day off under the sun and the blooms around him. Mona is sitting in one of the decorative tables in the garden, tending a pot of rose in front of her. The girl beamed radiantly at him and lowered her head as respect. In a few days, she will become her daughter. He smiled contentedly.

"I never knew you are gifted with a green thumb." William praised her.The girl lowered her head shyly.

"Granny taught me most about gardening, and I happen to enjoy it. My Gran's a super green thumb, that's for sure." Mona replied, continuing her work with the roses.

William laughed. Mona could have been his daughter if only fate wasn't that cruel. Or if only he wasn't a coward before. Twenty two years and still, William has too many what ifs.

"Bruce!" Miranda called Bruce, her personal assistant. The latter immediately turned to her.

"Yes, Luna?" Bruce answered. Bruce has been Miranda's assistant even when she was still a maiden at her own pack. She took Bruce with her when William removed her from her family as she became his mate. Away from the comforts of her home and with the presence of strangers, Miranda never felt at home. Bruce made her feel somehow, secure.

As the first child of Alpha Luke Redwood of the Scarlet Moon Pack, Miranda was supposed to be the heiress of their pack, but because she was a girl, her role was not to lead but to serve her mate. Then her brother, Mikhael was born and all her claims run down the drain. The moment he came, she was disregarded by both of her parents. Mikhael became the center of their world. Growing up, Mikhael always get her parents favor and affection, whereas she was given a nanny to attend to all her needs. Disregarded and unloved, that's how Miranda felt living under the roof of her parents. She's more than just a girl who would be taken by her mate one day, and will be his mate's possession. She longs for her parents' attention and love, which was selfishly refused to her. So, all her life she waited for her mate. She believed that only him can give her all the love she needed and she will gladly serve and love him with all of her heart in return.

And then William Jones came along. It was her father's funeral and pack leaders all over the land came to pay their last respects. William was with his father, and the moment she saw him, he immediately had taken Miranda's heart away. She was happy that her mate wasn't just a common man but a distinguished bachelor from another pack, a future Alpha at that. William was the answer to all of her prayers and she would not trade it for anything. But Miranda can't deny too, that William was indifferent to her. If it wasn't for the mate bond, she knew he won't even spare her his attention. He was even hesitant to accept her as his mate and she had no idea why. Her self-doubt, self-pity and insecurities was getting the best of her.

Somehow, she was taken to the Black Moon Pack just after her father was buried. Her Mother was still grieving for her father, did not even gave her a damn. Her brother was too pleased and eager to send her out of the way. She was apprehensive but Miranda knew better than that. She will be a Luna of a great pack, and she will have responsibilities to her mate and her new pack. She promised herself to love her mate with all her heart and that their children will be loved even more and will never suffer the same way as she did.

William was gentle and kind yet different. He might not say it but she can feel that she was not the one he wanted. Not long, she learned that William was in love with another girl. No. Was still in love with the girl he was supposed to marry before her. And it broke her heart and from then on, was drowned with bitterness and jealousy.

"I saw him in the garden a while ago. Smoking his pipe." Bruce aptly reported. She walked towards the garden and there she saw him laughing with Mona. She gritted her teeth, her inner self screaming with rage.

"Your mother was a fine woman, you know." William started, puffing smoke from his pipe.

"And so I heard. I think she was a very likeable person too..." Mona added, smiling to him. William felt sad seeing her smile. Or better yet, he still longs for her.

"Yes, she was. She's like a warm sunshine in the middle of winter. A ray of hope in a dreary day." William sighed, his old feelings once more taking a shot. Mona looked at him.

"Pardon me Alpha, but I also heard that you and my Mom were involved romantically?" Mona said silently, smiling meekly.

The Alpha laughed out loud. He looked like a boisterous young boy as he laughed. "Who told you that?" he replied after his laughters

"Mrs. Wilson told me when I visited her at her home last time."

"Ahh yes. Joey, your mother's bestfriend. Did you know that we were best childhood buddies? Of course. And yes, I will not deny What she said were true." was his answer as he bring himself to sit opposite to Mona.

"So it is true that you almost married my mother?!" Mona shouldn't be surprised, but she still is. The Alpha nodded still grinning, his pipe in between his teeth.

"Wow. It's amazing!" she exclaimed.

"And now, you will marry my son! This is more amazing right?" William grinned, looking at her. Thinking that his son and Mona will continue the love that he and her Mom had started more than two decades ago.

"Yes. It's amazing..." was Mona's only reply.

"I loved your mother. Very deeply. She was the best thing that ever happened to me, I thought we will end up together. But fate has other plans for us. I want you to know that we ended our relationship with a light heart and full understanding. I have responsibilities for my mate, and so she is. We became friends after that."

"I'm glad you did work out well even after what happened. " Mona uttered.

"Yes. It is because we knew the risks. We were aware of the risks and consequences that could happen if we continue our relationship. But we were young, stubborn and free. Still I can say those were the best times of our lives..." he said proudly. Mona is in awe knowing this side of her mother. Breaking rules, courage in loving someone who isn't for you, and setting the one you love for the common good.

"But you know," the Alpha's tone became sad and serious. "Some great love never dies. She has claimed a spot here in my heart. And there she will forever stay." The Alpha said sadly, pointing at his chest where his heart lays. She was dumbstruck, these were Mrs. Wilson's words. So, her mother was the Alpha's one great love? Is it? She looked at him still in disbelief. He smiled kindly and nodded, like a loving father to his daughter. He stood up and spoke behind his back.

"Yes. She is. My one great love. And I am glad it's her." he said before he left her alone in the garden of roses.

Miranda heard everything that he said. William has never forgotten her! How could he? She had given him all her love, served him with all her heart, placed him above everything else and yet, Claire has occupied what's supposed to be hers! How many times had she cried bitter tears for William? How many times is she willing to gamble herself to a man who never sees her worth? Angry tears, bitter tears, jealous tears. All these tears have flowed in her face already. In the eyes of her parents, she was worthless, in the eyes of her mate, she was not enough. Miranda choked her tears. This has to stop. Now.

Mona was walking to her room, humming a song. Her conversation with the Alpha has lighten her mood. She sighed admiring the Alpha's undying devotion to her Mom. Never have she known any man who is capable of loving as much as him, except her Dad whom she knows loves her mother above anything else. She end up sighing, men will be men. She reached her room and about to turn the knob when a hand of steel gripped her arm and pulled her harshly dragging her along. She looked at the owner of the arm and saw Bruce, the Luna's assistant. He has has that furious and dark look in his eyes. He dragged her to the basement.

"What's wrong Mr. Bruce? What is it?? You are hurting me!" He did not respond but dragged her harder to the basement. She starts to panic. What is happening to him? Has he gone mad. By the look in his face, she's sure he is truly mad.

He opened a door in the basement and throw her in. It was dark and damp in there. He locked the door and left her in that room. She ran to the door and knocked as hard as she can. Screaming for help hoping someone may hear. She banged the door, but it did not even gave a shudder. It is made of fine hardwood, her human bones will surely break if she force herself into it.

"Let me out!! Let me out!!!! " she screamed at the top of her lungs.

"Troy! Troooooyyyy!! Heeeellllppp!!! Tristannn!! TRISTAN!!! " she cried louder until she's out of breath, she knelt on the damp floor.

A spark of idea came to her. Her wolf! She can help her!

"Thalia...Thalia!" she concentrated, calling her wolf in her mind. Rivulets of perspiration are rolling down her forehead. She shut her eyes fiercely, focusing deeply.

"Please Thalia. Come to me. Speak to me... Thalia!!!" she opened her eyes. No one answered her. Not a ghost. Not a sound. Not even the slightest wind. Her wolf was silent.

She stayed in that position for a long time. The dampness of the sorrounding seeping through her clothes. Then there was a clang. The door opened. A torch came through lightening the corners of the room she's in. She closed her eyes because of the torch's brightness. When she finally opened her eyes, she saw her. The Luna walking towards her.

"Luna, Luna. Help me!" she reached for her. "Bruce. It's Bruce. He locked me in here..." she cried, panic in her eyes. Miranda did not bulge in her feet. Instead, Mona heard the loudest slap she ever heard in her life. Moments later she felt a burning sensation on her face and she's hugging the damp floor. A tickle of blood flowed from her nose. The Luna slapped her. She looked at her with accusing eyes.

"Luna? What have I done?"

"You are a curse!!!! You must not live!" Miranda's voice shuddered her. Mona felt fear ran in her spine. The Luna looked rabid and insane. Her eyes were wild with fury and a very hateful emotion Mona cannot place is written all over the Luna's face. She started to scratched her face, kicked her, slapped her some more, pulled her hair. She really don't know why the Luna is hitting her like a sworn enemy.

"Stooop Luna! Noooo... " she screamed as her body receives her every blow. A slap here, a pull there, and kick here and there. She's heaving for air, her lungs are failing her. She coughed and recoiled in the corner.

"What have I done to you Luna? Why are you doing this to me?? Tell me!" she demanded amidst her nonstop coughing and gasping for air.

"Because I hate your mother! And I despise you because you are your mother's daughter!!! She took everything that is mine. And you are do-ing the same!I abhor every inch of you!! Curse you!!!! " Miranda. pulled Mona's hair tight. The younger woman screamed of pain. "Bruce!!!" she called. The man came to her side and he gave her a air of scissors.

"I'll make sure that you will regret you ever came across me. I'll start with this hair!" Miranda hatefully snipped Mona's hair in every angle. Mona pleads and cried. Strands of hair are falling to the floor.

"Where is your wolf? Show it to me! Show it to me and I'll kill it!!!" Miranda said rabidly. Her eyes ready to kill. She pointed the scissors in Mona's face making it glide across her cheek, blood started to came out of it.

"Stop it!!!!" Mona was enraged and in pain, she pushed and scratched Miranda's chest, the Luna fell back. She looked at her hand and saw bloody claws as sharp as knives. She saw the Luna's chest and it was bleeding profusely. Miranda was in shock. And so was Mona.

"How dare you attack me! I am Miranda Redwood-Jones, the Luna of the Black Moon Pack, swears that you will pay this with your life!!!" With that, Bruce and Miranda shifted into their wolf form and attacked Mona simultaneously. They were the ferocious and rabid predators, up for the kill. And this time, Mona is their prey.

The Tale of the Moon

A long time ago, the moon goddess got tired of staying in her moon castle in the skies, guarding the world at night. So she decided to come down to the earth in the form of a maiden. together with her spirit animal - the wolf. The moon maiden lived in the realm of the mortal men contentedly and happily. Not long, a valiant man pursued the maiden and she fell in love with him. She gave him bounties imaginable and the purest of all love. The maiden and the man were happy. But not for long, the mortal man, as human nature, frail and easily corrupted, turned greedy and uncontented upon knowing that his lady was not an ordinary woman. He asked for more wealth, demanded power and immortality. The maiden refused his demands and with his dagger, he plunged it down to the maiden's heart. The maiden died, and her spirit animal howled to the moon. The moon goddess resurrected herself from the maiden's body and was furious of her lover's betrayal. She commanded her wolf to attack her man. The wolf complied and bit the man and with the moon goddess' curse, the man will turn to a beast every time the moon rises at its peak. Henceforth and forevermore, he became the very first werewolf. The Moon Goddess ascended to her castle in the skies and returned to guard the night skies. Upon her return, the Sun God seized the opportunity as he proclaimed his love for the Moon Goddess, emphasizing that a mortal was never fitting to the likes of them. The Moon Goddess agreed and they got married and took their dominion in the skies.

But the Moon Goddess' heart remained down on the Earth. Amidst the betrayal, she still longed for the mortal man, who was now a beast. She will always looked down on Earth to see him and everyday she will see demise, savagery and death from the werewolves. They killed each other as they claim territories. Brutally slayed the innocent and turned as many mortal beings into their kind.

One night, when the moon was asleep, the man whom the goddess loved, prayed fervently to her, begging for forgiveness. The life of the beast was a torture to him, he wanted to die but cannot for with the beast came longevity. The Moon Goddess having the kindest heart and the purest love in all beings, with the remaining love in her heart, once more pitied the man. She sent him a gift. The Moon Stone.

The Moon Stone will keep their kind tamed. This will give them power to shift into their werewolf form even the moon was out. The moon stone gave them power to control their wolves within them and let their human mind prevail even if they are in their wolf form. The Moon Stone purified their hearts and unleash the evil within them. From then on, the werewolves were tamed and worshipped the Moon Goddess for her mercy and love for them. The Moon Stone was kept in an ancient willow tree, deep in the Moon Forest. It stayed on Earth to keep the werewolves tamed and in control of themselves. Until today, the wolf howls to the moon to send his song of thanks, love and regret. Hoping it will reach the Moon Goddess above. Then, the Earth was once again in peace.

Now, the Sun God was very jealous of the werewolves, he sent his spirit animal - the fox - to ravage the earth and have them all killed. The Moon Goddess stopped the Sun of his plans, in return of her promise to give him a son. Later, the goddess gave birth to a celestial child, their son. He grew up into a fine young man in their castle in the skies. Every once in a while, he will sneak down to Earth and play his tricks among the mortals and the werewolves. Soon enough, he fell in love to the most beautiful maiden on Earth, a werewolf she was. Upon learning this, the Sun God threw him to the Earth and strip all of his son's powers. The Moon Goddess was once again heartbroken for the loss of her child.

Down on Earth, the maiden and the celestial man got married and they gave birth to a lovely girl. The girl grew up to be a beautiful maiden but within her, the essence of the moon and the sun was contained - the celestial beast, the fiercest and strongest beast among others - a nine tailed fox. The girl soon came of age and her beast awakened , she wasn't able to control it. It ravaged her pack, killing everyone including her parents. It's power was beyond measure and totally devastating. The world became grim and dark. The Moon Goddess came down to the Earth to destroy the beast once and for all, using the moon stone and her own powers. The moon goddess almost died battling with the beast, if only her husband- the Sun God - did not help her. Together, the celestial beast was overpowered and destroyed. And that was the last time the Moon Goddess set foot on Earth. Some said, she had exhausted her powers. Others said, she was imprisoned by the Sun God to stop her from looking down on Earth, and some said, she wasted away pining for the loss of her son. However, it was also believed that the celestial beast will come in power once more as long as the celestial child's bloodline is alive. As long as the descendants of the moon and the sun roams the earth, it will live.

Tristan closed the old dusty book - the Tale of the Moon. He didn't know how he came across this old book in their study, he was just looking for something else yet he found this. He stood up and think about the old tale. Since childhood, this folktale was told to them as a bedtime story, to scare children to sleep. But for Tristan, he understood it more deeply now.

Whether accurate or not, he knows that he must be ready, they must be ready in case the celestial beast returns.

And on this night, the celestial beast came back to life.

The Celestial Beast

Mona saw blood dripping to the floor. Her own blood mixed with saliva and sweat. She can hear Miranda's evil laughters and Bruce's vicious growling. Her sight, on the other hand, is blurry. She has wounds in varying depths and lashes all over her body. She lay crumpled on the floor, heaving deep breaths. She begged her wolf for help but it was silent. Have Thalia abandoned her? A new kind of helplessness and hatred is brewing in her heart. Hatred for deserving this kind of treatment. Helplessness for not being able to fight back. The Luna will definitely kill her this time, with an unforgiving look on her face, she never thought she'll survive. She thought she will be able to transform when she scratched Miranda awhile ago, but she was wrong. The claws vanished as fast as it came. Her body, deeply wounded and battered has turned numb after receiving too many blows. She ceased feeling the pain after being helpless. At last, Mona just wished to die. May the Moon Goddess take her for she have lost her will to live. She closed her eyes and let darkness embrace her.

It was the dead of the night when all others were asleep. Tristan was still awake, standing on the veranda feeling the chilly night air on his skin. Tomorrow, he will be wed. He thought of Mona and his confused emotions. The kiss they shared in the clearing delighted and brought him a wjole new feeling. Though, he still can't pinpoint the random feeling that rushed to his system. He has an idea what it is but it is too early yet to confirm. It is not fair for both of them. They are still yearning for their supposed-to-be-mates, especially him. The remnants of the broken bond still has influence in them, and recognizing new feelings between them is unjust. He sighed.

"Sleep trouble, eh?" His father, the Alpha speaks behind him. His pipe is smoking, and he is puffing out smoke. "Or pre-wedding blues?" He felt his father's hand tap his shoulder as he stand beside him, leaning on the railing.

"No, Dad. I'm just thinking." Tristan said silently.

"About what?" William inquires, puffing smoke from his pipe.

"About things... " he shrugs and hold the railing tightly.

"Having second thoughts??" William teased. He grins.

"No. Not that. But yeah. Somehow." he heaved a sigh, he is truly confused. "Maybe I was wrong in rushing into marriage after being rejected. Maybe I should have sort my feelings first before I dragged someone else into my own mess. It's unfair for her..." he answered silently, his words filled with thoughts.

"Maybe it's wrong. Maybe it's just right. But who knows? We really don't actually know anything? All I know is there's nothing wrong when it comes to love, son. If it's love, everything will simply have to fall right into place... " William simply said, blowing smoke from his mouth. Tristan's eyebrow raised. His father laughed cheekily.

"Say Dad, I know I am in no position to ask this, but I still want to ask." he hesitated and chuckled at the same time.

"What is it Son?" The Alpha replied simply, looking up at the bright moon.

"Have you ever loved a woman before? I mean, aside from Mom?" Tristan inquired slowly.

William gripped the railing tightly and cleared his throat before he answered him. "Yes. I did love someone else other than your mother. She was the woman I wanted to spend my life with. We almost got married." He chuckled as he looked directly in his son's eyes and he saw Tristan's bewilderment. Maybe he was not expecting his answer.

"What happened?" Tristan inquired.

"I found my mate. Your Mom." he puffed out a smoke.

"And her?" Tristan curiously asked.

"She found her mate too. And we end up marrying the mate fated for us. And with that we fulfilled the responsibilities to our destined mates..."

"Have you forgotten her. I mean, easily?"

"To be honest, to forget her was like trodding in hell. It was difficult and it pains me so much but I have to fulfill my responsibilities with your Mom. Maybe I am unfair with your Mom, she loved me wholeheartedly but I love her with only the love that's left from loving someone else. But I don't want to lie to myself that after all this years, I still have that constant longing for her. It was like a hole that no one else can fill." The Alpha said sadly. Now, Tristan understands his mother's stringy behaviors. Sometimes she's firm and cold and possessive towards his father and him. She has that temperament that he don't want to deal with if possible. Because his mother, even she became the Luna of the pack, cannot fill the emptiness in his father's heart and will never fill it no matter what she do.

"Don't hate me for this son. But I am just being honest with myself. And don't get me wrong. I love your Mom. She is my wife and I love her even more when she gave you to me." He smiled wistfully. "I did my best to make her happy and loved, but I know, she never is contented with the love I gave..."

"That is why, I am telling you this. If you love her, go for it. Let her feel it, tell her. Never waste a moment wondering why and what if. Love her with all the love you have because you'll never know what tomorrow will bring. Maybe today she's here, and tomorrow she's gone. I don't want you to regret the words you could have said and could have changed everything. " The alpha said wisely, it struck Tristan directly to his heart.

"What's with that look? I know how love looks like when I saw it. And I am seeing it in you." William squeezed Tristan's shoulder. In the moonlight, he can see his son's utter disbelief. One day, he himself will be able to recognize it. But he hoped that he won't take forever to understand what he truly feels.

"Well, I'll go back to sleep. You should also sleep. Tomorrow's your wedding day..." He winked at his son as he step away from him.

Tristan just shook his head with the thought. But his father is right, he needs to sleep. With one last look at the moon, Tristan steps away to his quarters.

A piercing scream broke through the night. Suddenly all of his senses were alert. His eyes immediately scanned the sorroundings. "What is it?" he whispered.

Troy was looking for Mona since he returned to the Manor. He had not seen her and it gave him a bad feeling. He scanned the entire Manor and failed to find her. He was in the kitchen when he heard laughters and growls from the basement. He went there and he saw Mona, lying bloody and crumpled on the floor, almost unconcious. He also saw the wolf-forms of Miranda and Bruce, circling her, ready for another attack.

"What is the meaning of this, Luna?!?" Troy yelled at Miranda. He saw the Luna looking very vicious it send shivers to Troy's spine.

"Here comes the great body guard! What a shame, guess you're too late!" the Luna yelled back, saliva falling from her mouth.

"Do you realize what you two have done!?" Troy was angry, he went to Mona and collected her. Her body was cold and listless, she was unconcious. His hand touched her hair now cut unevenly, one side of her head was almost shaved. Troy felt pity and regret for Mona. And he was too furious for what they did to her. This time, he would definitely will not hold back. He'll kill them!

"How touching?!" Miranda exclaimed. She give Bruce a knowing look and the latter nods on what to do.

"Mona, wake up. Can you hear me? Mona... " He called her name but she did not respond. Bruce attacked him while trying to wake Mona up, tearing his flesh. He shifted to his wolf form and an grim fighting between two wolves ensued.

Miranda was about to tackle Mona but she was rooted on the stop. Mona who was still unconcious, eerily stood up and floated in the air, her unevenly-cutted hair swaying upwards, she was then covered with a very bright light. Her eyes suddenly opened and purple lights were coming out of it. Then she let out a terrifying scream. The room shook and was then filled with cold wind, she was still covered with the bright light,her brown hair was the only thing visible and slowly the white light is starting to creep from the roots to the ends of her hair until she became a ball of blinding yellow light. It took only seconds but for them, it seemed like a long time. From the light stepped a magnificient and marvelous beast Troy had known only in legends. A snow-white nine-tailed fox covered in a yellow light as yellow as the moon's gleam above, so huge it reached the basement's ceiling. It was magnificient and terrifying, emitting a danherous aura. Miranda and Bruce cowered in fear, Troy himself was rooted on the spot. It's purple eyes were furious, and with a blink of an eye, Miranda and Bruce lay facedown, unconcious on the floor. It growled and the ceiling exploded and the night sky was then visible. It flew up, so high as if kissing the moon.

Not long after the echoing scream, something exploded in the Manor's groundfloor. Tristan ran to the end of the veranda and saw a ruined ground floor. From it, a shining yellow light spurted to the sky. Tristan cannot believe what he had seen but it is real and it was here. It flew straight to the moon as it let out a cry. The celestial beast has risen.

The Legacy of the Horn

n explosion erupted in the night. Tristan and William sensed immense danger around. And from the source of explosion, came the beast that Tristan just read from the old dusty book from the study. The celestial beast flying to the sky and it gave a cry so terrifying everything shuddered. The Celestial Beast came back to life.

Then a blaring horn came off, alerting all of the Black Moon Pack and all nearby packs.

The horn means a warning to evacuate the elders, sick and unable and the children to a safe place. All the pack warriors and able pack members are to aid in this emergency. The horn was never blown over centuries, in fact, this is the first time it blared which only means that the Black Moon Pack is in grave danger.

The rising of the legendary beast deserves a full-scale alert that nearby packs will be alerted too. Later, a stronghold of warriors from allied packs will come rushing to help. The horn does not only serve as a warning but also it symbolizes the unity of the entire werewolf race, that once blown from whichever pack, misunderstandings and conflicts will be set aside and all will held hands to help one another. This made the werewolf race a stronghold - they are united in times of disasters and crisis. Eversince the first of their kind was forgiven by the Moon Goddess, they pledge to have each others back in times of grave danger. And today, the legacy is served in a golden platter.

William has to act fast, his pack are all gathered and he immediately gave the commands. Secure the old, sick and children, she-wolves as first-aiders and warriors on guard. They had numerous drills making his pack in full alert and all in stance to fight. The legendary enemy has returned and it proved to be ferocious, fearless and vicious. As it came down, it started to ravage the place. With it's breath came death. With a whip of one of its tail came chaos. Explosions, fire, thunderous howls and more chaos was painted all around. The houses and establishments came tumbling one by one.

The warriors fight back bravely but in every growl of the beast they were thrown away. As large, formidable and evil, it was.

"MONA!!!! MONAA!! STOP IT!" Troy shouted, begging the beast to stop. He was running in front of it, he was bloody himself. Troy shifted to his wolf form but the beast shrieks and Troy was thrown away to a wall so hard it broke. He was buried in debris. She-wolves rushed to help him.

Tristan is trying to process Troy's words. The beast is Mona? Tristan can't believe his ears. Then a yell echoed in the area.

"She's a curse! I told you!!!I told all of you!! That girl is a curse!!" It was Miranda, his mother, shouting at the top of her lungs. Surfacing from the ruins, she is back in her human form, bloody, naked and barely alive. He ran to her.

"Kill her! Destroy the girl!! Save the pack! DESTROY HER!" she screamed wildly, her irises as small as a dot and eyes were furious , wild and blodshot. She coughed blood nonstop and then she fell unconcious in Tristan's arms.

"Help! Medic! Help the Luna!" Tristan yelled for help. The medic immediately gathered to attend to their Luna. Her breathing was slow and ragged. Tristan is worried in her mother's situation.

Mona is encased within the beast's body. It feels warm and light, soft and fuzzy. All her pain was wiped, her wounds healed and she feels brand new. The feeling was wondrous, nudging her to close her eyes and savor the beautiful feeling.

She heard a lovely voice, it was her mother's voice. She appeared in front of her, very alive and well, smiling lovingly at her. She can't believe she is seeing her right now.

"Mom?" she has tears in her eyes.

"It's me, my darling..." Claire embraced her. She thought this must be a dream but how come she can feel her warmth, her steady breathing and her beating heart? She returned the embrace tighter.

"I only dreamt about this and here it is." She feel her mother's warmth and sweet scent.

"I missed you, my darling. " Said Claire's sweet voice. Mona closed her eyes and savored the moment, hugging her mother for the first time and not wanting her to go.

"I want to stay like this with you, forever... " she whispered as she looked at her face, memorizing every detail of her face.

"Of course, you can. From this day on, you will stay with me. I wont ever leave you. I will be by your side to protect you. You will never be alone, not anymore... " Claire said tenderly. "I love you my dearest.."

Mona just snuggled closely to her mom. The latter pats her head and hums a lullaby. It was so comfortable, sweet and it was all she ever wanted.

"I always wanted to stay with you, be by your side and watch you grow day by day..." Claire continued softly, "But fate did not want me to.. And I can't fight against the will of the Gods..."

"Though, I am here now. This time, I will never let you go, my sweet child." she continued patting Mona's head as she lull her to sleep. Mona smiled, how she yearned for this!

The wolves kept attacking the beast but it seemed to be useless. It seemed to be invulnerable, only with every attack, it strikes harder and fiercer. Too many of their pack warriors were wounded, some were dead. Parts of the town was on fire and destroyed. Still, it trampled and ravaged some more. Troy never stopped attacking the beast. Doing his best to save her, hoping to wake Mona up. He will not let the beast devour her.

As the Alpha gathered his men and their weapons, the back up from the other packs arrived. Giving them hope, especially that hey are already outnumbered. The Alphas from the other pack came too and they need to strategize. William gathered the other Alphas and briefed them of the situation.

"The Celestial beast has risen. It was contained in a girl's body." William started.

"Too many of my men were already wounded, some had died. Half of the town is in ruins and it never stopped its rampage."

"Who is the vessel of the beast?" Asked Arthur Mills, the Alpha of the Golden Moon Pack.

"It's Mona Mayfield. Bill's daughter, my Beta here, and my son's bride-to -be..." William directly answered.

"Did you know that she is the vessel?" Asked the Grey Moon's Alpha, Rick Rogers.

"No. That we have no idea of until today." He answered firmly.

"I heard from my sister that you have a cursed child here. The girl with the silver hair and mismatched eyes? Isnt she the vessel?" Mikhael Redwood, Alpha of the Scarlet Moon Pack asked arrogantly. He has the same bad temper as his sister Miranda.

"Yes. It is her. But we don't know what she is--"

"You should have listened to my sister to kill that cursed child! If only you have killed her when she's young, we should not be in this dilemma!" Mikhael cut William's words.

Bill was just in the side, listening but grim. Upon hearing the Scarlet Moon's Alpha, he wasnt able to hold it anymore, he stomped his way to him and grabbed the collar of his shirt.

"She is my daughter! My child! My flesh and blood that you want to kill!!" Bill said in gritted teeth, eyes furious. "And how could you kill an innocent child?! Is that your way in your pack? Killing innocent helpless children? "

"As if you have been a good father to her! You had neglected and mistreated her remember? So what's with the fuss? You should have just killed her before and we shouldnt be here today!! What is one life against thousands or worse, the death of our kind? " Mikhael spat back.

"I have my mistakes and I am have regretted all of it. Maybe I wasnt a perfect father and I disliked her as a child, but never have I thought of killing her!!" Bill said furiously.

William grabbed Bill urging him to stop. "Bill please, calm down. And same as you Alpha Mikhael! This is not the time to argue!" he scolded and successfully parted the two men who was trying to bite each other's neck.

"Gentlemen, we have to maintain our composure and stop acting like children. We are facing a dreadful dilemma right now and if it will not be acted upon, will surely lead to our demise!" The Grand Alpha Lourd Holmes firmly said. He is old yet very wise. He has been into lots of battles in his prime and an undeniable strategist and highly respectable leader.

"We have to help one another to defeat our common foe. For our people. For the survival of our kind!" The Grand Alpha added. His voice thundering in the hall. Everyone kept their mouth shut, not trying to anger the Grand Alpha once more.

"Now, let us discuss how can we defeat this beast."

"If we recall the Tale of the Moon, it was the Moon Goddess who defeated the Celestial beast, with the aid of the Sun God. We don't have the moon goddess now. I mean, it has been ages since she last trodden the Earth and there's no way she will come down to save us." The youngest Alpha spoke, Theo Thomas of the Amber Moon Pack.

"What are you implying Alpha Theo? That we don't have the power to overcome this foe? That only the Moon Goddess can save us?!? " Alpha Mikhael chirped in, still in his arrogant tone.

"I'm afraid yes. The beast is formidable. Silver bullets, wolfsbane arrows, and other weapons will not harm it, it is unlike us. It is the beast that came out from the essence of the Moon and the Sun. Maybe it will affect her, our weapons but only for a moment. Our weapons cannot destroy her..."

"You are correct, I'm afraid we have few options here or none. Fighting one on one is futile, with its magnificence and outworldly strenght, surely we will be overwhelmed." The Grand Alpha spoke gloomily.

"But we have another way and I think, we will have a chance."Theo added, feeling excited of his words.

"Say it Alpha Theo." William eagerly nudged, wanting to stop this as soon as possible.

"The Moon Stone" Theo said as if a whisper.

Claire can see her daughter, comfortably nestled in her chest. She kissed the top of her forehead and played with her hair. It has turned back to what it was, her silver-blonde hair with brown strands in its silky long splendor. She whispered softly in Mona's ear.

"This time, no one will hurt you. They trampled on you, humiliated you, made you an outcast for so long. You have suffered enough my child. This time, they will pay. They will pay... " Claire said in gritted teeth, her eyes gleaming with hatred.

The beast has caused too much havoc, it has almost reduced the entire town to ruins. As legendary as it is, proving to be more powerful and destructive than the legends. The Black Moon Pack is in the brink of death and no horn can ever stop that now.

Do or Die

"The Moon Stone?" Mikhael asked.

"Yes." Theo looked at all the Alphas in the room. All were serious and are waiting for his next words.

"It is said that the Goddess overpowered the beast with the power of the moon stone. And it has the closest thing to the goddess, it came from her. So, I believe it will help.. "

"But come to think of it, maybe it is our last card. But the Moon Stone holds the power to keep us different from monsters. Say we take the moon stone, what will happen to us then? Either, we will defeat the beast or we will turn to untamed monsters again. We cannot do it." The Grey Moon Alpha, Rick Rogers spoke, weighing all his words.

"Has anyone of you have seen the moon stone before? Was it kept hidden deep in the heart of the Moon Forest? No one has ever stepped on the sacred forest since the Goddess placed it there." Another Alpha expressed his doubts.

The room was then filled with clamor as each of them expressed their opinions. The Grand Alpha cleared his throat.

"We will not finish this if we will talk at the same time! Let us come down to consensus before my town turned to dust!" Alpha William firmly said, the other men stopped talking and once again were in attention.

"I agree." The Grand Alpha interjected "Let's hear the plan..."

The Alphas listened as Theo lay out the plan. And everyone nod their head in agreement.

"I've seen the moon stone." Alpha Theo began nervously. All eyes were on him, both in confusion and doubt.

"When I was twelve, my father and our pack Elder went to the Sacred Moon Forest to send our prayers because my twin sister Thea was dying of a grave disease. We grew up together and I can't imagine my sister to just die like that. So, an idea struck me. When the Great Elder and my father was not looking, I took a bit of the Moon Stone, pulverized it and mixed it with my sister's medicine. I--I made her drink the medicine with the moon stone powder and it worked! Like a miracle, my sister was healed and not long, she's back in perfect health! It saved my sister!!"

A hush of accusations erupted in the room.

"You defiled the Moon Stone!! You disrespected it! You stole it!" one Alpha points at him angrily.

"My sister was dying!! She could have been dead eight years ago but the Moon Stone saved her and I am proud that I did it! It was for a good cause, and I took just a tiny bit, pea-size..." Theo defended at the men in the room.

"We will just take a chunk of the Moon Stone. Pulverize it and sprinkle to our weapons. Maybe it will save us just like how it saved my sister."

The men fell silent.

"Let's do this! This is our only shot. Grand Alpha, please delegate." Alpha William politely bowed to the Grand Alpha.

The Grand Alpha cleared his throat before he begins.

"We will need the fastest trackers in the land, Arthur Mills, Theo Thomas, Ken Edwards. Collect a chunk of the Moon stone in the Sacred Moon Forest. How long should we wait until you return?"

"With our rate, three hours Grand Alpha... " Arthur Mills estimated.

"Too long. Make it two hours!"The men nodded firmly.

"Mikhael Redwood, Diego Summers, and Keith Michaels, procure all the firearms and weapons and bring them here."

"Yes, Grand Alpha!!"

"The other Alphas, gather your men in the grounds. Don't let them engage in the fighting yet. We will wait until the trackers comes back with the moon stone. This is to reduce our casualties. For the mean time, we will hold the beast down."

"William Jones, you will be my second in command." The Grand Alpha finished delegating his men.

"Let's do this and defeat the beast!" He said firmly. Then the men in the room salutes and proceed to their respective missions.

The beast was rampaging the town center now. The warriors did not waste more time, they took out the silver chains, praying it will hold the beast down. With a giant sling shots, they flew the chains against the beast and tied the beast down. Soon, it was pinned to the ground. The beast shrieked and tried to shake off the chains. They continued encasing the beast in thick chains until it was almost covered. It is shaking the chains off and trying to remove the restraints, they are nervous that it wont hold much longer for some of the chains are starting to break off. But with each broken chain, another chain was added.

Each wolf came with wolfsbane serum and each injected the poison to the beast's body, making it limbs limp. Some shot it with weapons, wounding it. It growled, angrier than ever but the wounds are healing as fast as it came. It shrieked an ear-splitting cry that the chains broke off and everyone was thrown in a shockwave.

The next warriors repeated the attack, pinning the beast to the ground again. Some were firing at her, but its effects did not last just like the other weapons. But still, the efforts was not in vain, it slows the beast somehow, though it angers it more.

After two hours, the trackers came back with a piece of the moon stone. The Grand Alpha pulverized it, and sprinkled the moon stone powder to the weapons, arrows, spears, bullets, daggers and on every weapon on the floor.

The beast broke off the chain after it rested. Then it growled again, and on it's mouth, a fireball was forming. Seconds later, it flew and exploded ten miles away. It did it again and hit every target with it's fireball.

The warriors get in position armed with their weapon sprinkled with moon stone powder. A hit to the beast connected and it proves fatal. It flew up screaming of pain!

The moonstone is effective, it can damage her! Suddenly, all the wolves spirits' raised. They continued shooting at her and in every hit that connects, it gave a cry and returns a fireball. A giant spear was sent to tje skies and pierced the beast's hindleg, it lost it's balance and fell to the ground with a thundering thud. Bright purple lights are dissipating from the beast's wounds to the sky.

"Don't kill her!!! STOOOPP!!! Don't harm her!" Bill screamed. Running in front of the men in formation. William came to him to move him away.

"Bill what are you doing!" Alpha William intensely said.

"They might kill my daughter Alpha! They might kill her!!" he repeated, he is in obvious tension.

"Bill calm down. We have no other way. We will be wiped out if we let her loose." William said firmly. "There's no other way!"

"Then contain her, not kill her! Remember this?!" Bill showed his left arm in William's face. He looked down on his own hand and saw the silver threads shining again, covering his hand. Because of distress he forgot about this. He was struck again with dread.

The unbreakable bond is back and it means Mona is in danger. And they have to protect her or the bond's power will consume them. William has never been confused before.

Tristan's left hand is glowing, silvery thread are creeping from his finger tips to his forearm, leaving a tingling burning sensation.

"What is this?" Tristan whispered.

"An unbreakable bond! Someone you promised your protection is in danger, Young Master!" A wolf answered him.

"To whom did I promised my protection?" Tristan was bewildered, he has no idea about this. It glowed multiple times already since he was a child. Something struck him. A distant memory came back. He was eight and he once heard his parents arguing something about an unbreakable bond. His mother was very angry to his father for agreeing with a bond - the bond to protect the cursed child! That his father has dragged his bloodline for the sake of her! Was it Mona whom his father vowed his protection? Then it all came rushing to him, memories when his arm glowed. Most of it happens when Mona's life was in danger. And if he's right, it only means that he has a firmer reason to save her!

The beast cried and whipped one of its tail, it produced a whirlwind. The wolves under attack were blown away, throwing them to walls and buildings as far as a mile. Another tail whipped and debris, rocks and chunks of soil float and suddenly it is raining with debris, soil and rocks. The wolves hide to evade the attack. It cried again and Tristan knew that the beast is very furious now.

"Alpha, Grand Alpha. I beg you. Let me talk to her. I can calm her down. She is my daughter. Don't harm her anymore, she don't know what she's doing. Let me talk to her. She will listen to me." Bill kneeled in front of the Grand Alpha, begging him to hear him.

"We will rest the attack but we will be in stand-by. Go and talk to her." The Grand Alpha said powerfully.

"I also have a daughter. I know how it feels to lose one." He said grimly. "Go and save her. But if it you don't succeed, we have no other choice but to destroy her." Bill nodded firmly, determined and grateful that the Grand Alpha is giving him the one chance to save his daughter.

"I'll go with you." William volunteered. "I have a part in this. I must fulfill my vow." Bill nodded at him in agreement. They are more than just Alpha and Beta now, this time, they are brothers working for a common good.

Tristan met them in the doorway with Troy who was badly wounded and hurt.

"Let me help, Dad." Tristan forcefully said as he met his father and Bill. Troy follow suit. Bill stopped Troy, seeing the wounds he got.

"Troy, go get some help for yourself. You're hurt." Bill said to Troy, a look of worry in his eyes.

"I'm fine, Sir. I am her Guardian. I must be there for her." Troy answered without hesitation.

"Suit yourself, son." Bill replied. And the four of them marched towards the Celestial Beast now shrieking with fury. It's do or die.

Inner Demons

Mona felt sudden jolts from the blasts and with it came pain in various parts of her body. She woke up with a start, her mother still cradling her.

"They're hurting you again, my dear. Those imbeciles!" Her mother whispered harshly.

"Mom? What is happening??" Mona asked quizzically. The shots of pain in her body were grappling her. She fought and managed to stand.

"They are trying to kill you, Mona. Show them your power! Smite them! Make them pay!" Claire expressed hatefully. All of a sudden, Mona seemed to see her caring mother has turned to a different persona. A vile and hateful person. That is what she's seeing now.

"Mona!?! Mona! I know you're in there... " a voice called her. Deep and clear and strong. Her father's!

"Dad? is that you?" she called back but she can't see anything.

"Don't listen to! It's not your father Mona. It's a lie! Listen to me!" She grabbed her face so that their eyes meets. It was pitch black.

"He will lure you to lower your defenses then will strike at you! Kill them before it happens! Kill them or they'll kill you!" Her mother screamed at her face, Mona stepped back.

"Mona, please come back! Sweetheart, wake up! It's me, your Dad! Come back to us!!" Mona heared his father's voice, pleading.

She faced to where the voice is coming from and a part of thr wall clears out giving her a view of the outside world. There she saw her father, Alpha William, Troy and Tristan in front of her.

"Enough Mona. Come back now..." Bill said, his hands outstretched.

She swung her head around and saw destruction. Collapsed buildings, unrecognizable terrain, dead men around and the wounded being attend-ed by the medics. She backed down. Her knees suddenly lost its energy to stand up.

"Is this my doing?" She said terrified. Her mother stood behind her and whispered to her ear.

"Yes my sweet. You are bound to destroy them. Just like what the Luna had been saying. You did this and you should be proud!" Goosebumps rose in her body. The sight outside is terrifying plus the way her mother whispered in her ear. Mona cannot believe that she's hearing this from her mother.   Her town has been reduced to ruins, her pack dying because of her! She can't breath, she don't know what to do. She heard her father pleading at her to stop. But she can't feel her body, something is not right. Her mother speak up, holding both of her shoulders now, shaking her the life out of her.

"Don't listen to him! He is a liar. He will fool you and use you. He's just there because he will die if he won't do anything. The unbreakable bond is consuming him everytime they attack you. Which only means, when you die, he will die too. In fact, all of them are just pretending to help you, but the truth is, they are all afraid to die. Don't believe any of them! Destroy them!" Her mother said fiercely.

She shook her head and removed her mother's hands on her, unbelieving. She leaned on the wall, feeling tired and in disbelief. How could her mother say that to the men who loved her and to the pack that owned her? How could she? Claire approached her and whispered some more to her ear, totally corrupting her mind until a purple cloud sorrounds her and started draining her conciousness.

The beast seemed to listen to Bill. It stopped moving as if absorbing Bill's words, its features softening. Suddenly, it turned wild again, it swat Bill down under its paws, William was shoved aside, he was thrown three meters away. Troy and Tristan barely escaped. Spears were shot to the beast, making it wilder.

"Mona, don't do this! Please, you've done enough. You've destroyed much, you can't continue doing this. Don't let the beast control you! This is not who you are!" Bill shouted under his breath. Fighting against the weight of its paw crushing him. She is relentless and demonic, an unforgiving look on its face.

A giant arrow was shot and it directly hit the beast's shoulder. It let out a wild scream, releasing Bill. Troy immediately pulled Bill to safety, his breath shallow. The troop went on an attack frenzy, the beast tried to evade the attacks but some got lucky hits. Dissepating purple light oozed from the beast's wounds.

Mona can hear words but all in a blur, she can't clearly understand them. She seemed to be in a nightmare, she wants to wake but her eyes wont open. She's trapped.

"Listen to your heart..."

"Listen to your heart... "

"Listen to your heart... "

These words keep repeating in her mind. At the start was just like a whisper until it became audible.

"Kill them! Destroy them!! "

"Kill them! Destroy them!! "

"Kill them! Destroy them!! "

Another voice is whispering in her ear. It speaks louder, growling, threatening and terrifying Mona. She is getting more and more confused and anxious.

Her body is responding to the pain in every shot that hits her, plus the confusion in her mind, she feels helpless.

"You are not a beast Mona! You are my daughter!! Come back, you belong here with us..." Bill pleads some more, hoping she will hear him this time.

Claire appeared in front of her. Coaxing her to calm down, telling her that destroying everything is the only way.

"Why do you want me to destroy them? This is your town! They are your pack!" Mona said in a little voice, her face hidden in her palms. Her mother take her hands away her face and remove strands of hair on her face. Her hand lingering in her silver hair. Claire looked gloomy and sad.

"Remember when they told you that you are cursed because of your hair and these eyes? Remember how they look at you with disgust? When you were a child, those kids did not let you join their games - not even once, they don't even want to sit beside you in a bus... My poor girl, they played pranks and bullied you! Those girls who kept on snickering whenever you pass by, that man who rejected you and the other who took you in to save his ego and to add more to your miseries! How they neglected you, made you an outcast of the pack and almost kill you! You don't deserve all of those... They made you suffer. They hurt you. They blame you for every bad thing that has ever happened in the pack! Even the people whom I had entrusted to care and protect you had betrayed my trust! I have seen them all. I felt all your miseries too. And I cannot forgive them for that. It is time to make them miserable. Let them taste how bitter your life has been... Payback time, Mona. With hate, you will have more power. Hate them! Curse them! Make. Them. Pay!!!" Claire said with conviction, her eyes glassy with tears.

Memories came flooding back to Mona. The numerous times she was not treated fairly, how immediately she was blamed for the little things she had not done, swallowing anything they throw at her. Rejected all her life. Beaten, broken until she's bent. Fat tears raced down her face. The pain that she tried to bury deep in her heart are rushing out, bellowing waves after waves of pain and hatred.

"That's it Sweetie. Very good. Hate them some more and let's get this over with. They are all the same. They should not be forgiven..." Claire urged her some more. She screamed the pain away, releasing them as a cloud of dark smoke went out of her body and seeps through the walls where she is confined. Fueling the beast, giving it additional strength.

The beast gave out another terrifying cry as wounds after wounds are closing rapidly.

"She's healing herself!!" shouted one pack warrior. Attacks fly in the sky both from weapons and the warriors themselves - grappling, wounding, and taking the beast down. Pouring effort after effort, blood after blood. But their weapons are almost exhausted too, and the moon stone powder are all used up now. The warriors know what will happen next if they will not be able to take down the beast in time. It will destroy all of them to smithereens or devour them whole.

The Grand Alpha furrowed his forehead, it seems years has been added on his already snow-white hair. Burdened with this incredible dilemma and the loss of options in defeating the beast. Maybe the Sun God's dream of wiping out their kind is finally coming true. But one thing is sure, their kind will not settle down without a fight.

Through her Memories

It was getting dark again. The battle has been going on for twenty-four hours now and the warriors are exhausted. The best warriors among the packs were already tired and wounded. The beast is unstoppable and it has immeasurable strength. The Alphas themselves had engaged in the fight and even their incredible fighting skills are no match to that of the beast. This is expected to a celestial beast, only that, it's power is too overwhelming. Now that the weapons were exhausted and the moon powder gone, they were solely relying in their strength and battle prowess. But the pack is also a formidable foe, as stubborn and vicious, they are also united. Team work may be their ultimate weapon against their celestial opponent. Good thing that the news about the beast has spread, more reinforcements has arrived bringing with them more firearms, weapons and manpower.

The Grand Alpha has decided to chunk the moon stone in half which made the Black Moon Great Elder angry as it is a defilement to the Moon Goddess' gift to their kind. But having no more options, he just consented but it went through a series of arguments before he finally was convinced. They will have to deal with the consequences later.

Not a single building was left in the town. Houses, buildings, establishments were all blown to pieces as if a bomb was dropped on it. The children, old and disabled, including the wounded has to be evacuated in the nearest town of the Golden Moon pack. The town is now a battlefield. The ground zero of chaos.

Bill having been injured by the beast's attacks never stopped from trying to talk to his daughter. Something is manipulating her and the must help her. No matter how many times he was whacked, thrown, and torched by its fireballs, he will never give up. He will continue to reach for her. Bill now realizes those times when Mona was just a child who was trying to reach out to him, please him with her little achievements in school, and the way her eyes speaks affection for him only to be takenfor granted. Those times when he beats her for being the child who took his wife away, the child he neglected for sins she had no idea of and for being a reminder of the vow he broke the moment Claire died. This must be how Mona felt during those times. To be ignored no matter how many times you reach out for that one person. To be unnoticed no matter how much effort you give. To be unheard even if you are running out of voice calling for them. Indeed, the feeling is not funny. Now, he understands how it felt. Bill felt warm tears gushing in his face, bitter and angry tears for himself.

"Mona! Wake up! Please...." Bill begged crying, hugging the beast's gigantic leg. It stomped and stomped until Bill has lost his grip, he fell flat on the ground. With it's giant paw, it crushed Bill, forcing the life out of him.

William saw Bill in the brink of death, being crushed by the beast's giant paw as if a bug. He saw a fallen spear, still emitting a pinkish glow, bathe in moon stone powder. He took it and pierced through the beast's leg, it let out a scream, releasing Bill who was now as limp as wilted eggplant, blood dripping from his mouth, eyes wide open and dazed. Tristan helped him to move Bill away and give him away to the medical team.

William is terrified, the hard truth sinking in. Now that Bill is spent, who else can stop the beast??

The wolves exhibit their agility, agitating the beast because it can't seize them. Firearms are shot to the beast , slowing its movements.

"Don't let them frighten you, sweetie. You have the upper hand now, you have power beyond imagination and none of these weaklings can match you. This time, they will bow at you. They will recognize your power and they must accept their defeat!" Claire nudged her again.

"You are not a beast. You are one of us. Remember what you are!" a voice amplified in Mona's head. A voice she had known all her life, and she the one she had been missing.

"Granny?" she stopped and listened tl its echoes. It's Josephine's voice.

"Don't let the beast control you! Fight it!" another voice spoke, it was rather ragged and in much difficulty as if being trapped somewhere. She knows the whose voice it was.

"Thalia??" for the first time in a long time, she heard her. What happened to her? Why is she reaching out just now?

"Is that you? Thalia? Talk to me..." Mona pleads, hoping she is not just hearing and imagining things.

A puff of fog gingerly encircled her. The form of which was that of her wolf.

"Thalia??" she repeated.

"It's me Mona. It's me your wolf, Thalia..." Thalia spoke softly.

"What happened to you? Why did'nt you reached out to me? I thought you abandoned me..." Mona kneeled in front of her wolf.

"I will never do that. I will be with you always..." Thalia said, breathing heavily.

"Then what's wrong? Why can't I shift to your form and why have you stopped talking to me?" Mona demanded, her voice irritated.

"I was restricted and imprisoned. I was bound within. The power that bind me was so strong I can't break free..." Thalia explained sadly.

"Who bind you?" Mona asked quizzically, still not believing to what she's hearing. Is it possible that her own powers restricted her wolf from coming out? As she grew up, she knew she was different. The development of her senses and agility was beyond anyone in their generation though she had not used much of it. Has she developed another kind of power?

"The beast contained me Mona. The Celestial Beast." Thalia answered directly.

"What?!" Mona was surprised. That is impossible! How could she have such a beast in her?

"The beast wakes up after the rejection of our mate. It has been gaining power eversince. Taking power from your miseries that was buried deep in your heart. I can't overpower him. He is much, much stronger than me..." Thalia explained. Mona was still in shock.

"And it is ravaging the town. It has taken over you, feeding in your hatred. Destroying everything in its path." Mona shook her head in disbelief.

"My mom... She..." Mona cannot finish her words.

"She is a fake." a casual yet loving voice said. Now her puff of smoke of a wolf turned to another form that of Josephine.

"Granny!" Mona exclaimed and reached out to her, but as soon as she touched the fog it deformed like a placid water when disturbed.

The beast stopped moving as if contemplating, like a toy car that has ran out of batteries. The pack warriors waited for its next move, but it had not moved a muscle. Realizing that the beast is not in itself, the wolves took their chance to attack it and bound its feet in giant silver chains, the moon powder glowing on it. As soon as it was chained, he directed the warriors to stop attacking. Spears and arrows sticking all over its body. Lashes and wounds oozing with purple light evaporating to the heavens.

Tristan moved near to the beast's feet. He slowly touched it and as soon as he felt the beast's fur in the palm of his hand, something carried his soul somewhere, as if it was sucked out of his body. But his conciousness is intact though he feels drifting. He is lifted upwards until he stopped and saw himself in a long hallway. Both walls looked differently. The one in the right has bright and warm paint, the other on the left is dark with peeling paint, purple smoke hovering above. At the end of the hall is an old door, a bright light emanating from it. As he walked towards the door, the walls showed images as if a slide show. Images of days gone by, like muted video clips. The images were familiar but it was not his. Then he realized that the images were Mona's memories.

"She's a fake. It is the beast's way of controlling you. It makes use of your greatest desires and using your mother, as you can see is very effective. Don't let it control you Mona. You are more than that..." Josephine spoke clearly.

"I- I don't understand..." Mona said confusely. It means her mother was just an illusion created by the beast to manipulate her? She believed that finally she have someone to defend her, protect her and give her refuge. Realizing they were lies.

"Your mother has died Mona. She's never coming back. Remember that. There is no way she can be with you..." Josephine said firmly.

"Then what about you? Why are you here then? You're dead too. If what you said were true, then you must not be showing yourself to me. Are you ...some kind of a trick?" she said accusingly.

"I am not a trick, Mona. But I am not real as well. I am just a figment of your memories. You have known me all through your life. You loved me and I am here in your heart. Unlike your Mom, though you love her. You were not able to interact with her. You never seen her alive. She can't be part of your memories. And I, I am here in your heart. As I said, the beast used your Mom and your desire to meet her inorder to manipulate you..." The old woman explained gently, like a loving mother to her toddler who was throwing a tantrum.

"Don't believe her!!! She is a liar!!" Shouted Claire, who appeared out of the blue, standing behind Josephine. She clawed at the it hastily until Josephine's form turned to wisps of fog.

"She is deceiving you! Remember your revenge!" Claire said angrily.

A wisp of fog swirled near her ear leaving one last whisper before it vanished.

"Listen to your heart... Remember who you truly are...."

Tristan walked slowly, looking at each of the frozen moments on the wall. All of it were Mona's. From when she was a little girl up to now. He saw when she was beaten by her Dad who was so drunk. He smashed a vase on Mona's head, broken pieces scattering around, her head bleeding profusely. Little Mona retreated under the table to evade her father's wrath. Soon, an old woman came out removing the child away from her father who seem to have gone mad. Another was when her classmates were picking at her. Little Paula and Myrtle, pulling Mona's hair simultaneously, Burris were scattering the contents of Mona's bag. Excluding her in group works, avoiding her as if she's carrying a contagious disease. He noticed that these memories in the dark wall were her bad memories. She was consistently shoved, pushed aside or down to the mud, thrown with things, made her clean up other's mess and she just let them do it. Another was when Henry rejected her. She was totally broken although she managed to eventually accept all of it and keep on putting her brave face on. She stifles a cry but after will stand up and wipe her tears away. She is a very strong girl and he admire her for that.

On the other side of the wall, Tristan saw Mona smiling. He rarely see her smile, except one time and he thinks that it was the most beautiful thing he has ever seen. Her eyes smiles too when she smile, so charming, delightful and pure. How could he so blind? He saw her laughing with her Granny Josephine, tending the flowers, helping her in household chores,celebrating her birthdays with Josephine and later with Troy, or just plainly sitting with her. Tristan saw it all. She's happy too in her solitude. When she's sketching, running in the woods, gathering plants and insects, spending the night looking up at the moon with hopeful eyes. Memories of young Mona until she was her age now. She had her happy moments and this wall contains all of it. He stopped on two frame of memories that outshines the rest, one was when her father has finally begged for her forgiveness and started making amends. It was a rare and beautiful sight indeed. Another includes him and his heart suddenly went crazy. It was one of her precious memories. It was when he kissed her for the first time in the clearing. He can feel the rush of delight in his body, the very same as he felt during that time. He's elated knowing that his gesture made her happy. He moved on, the door a meter away from him. On the opposite wall another shining sad or bad memory loomed and he stopped on his tracks. He saw Mona, his mother and Bruce who were brutally torturing her until she lay crumpled on the floor, bloody and her spirits bent. His mother looking very evil, he had not thought she'll be able to do it to her. He can't watch any longer, it pains him to watch her that way and he is furious with his Mother. And then Mona transformed into a white ball of blinding light and from it emerged the celestial beast.

An ear-splitting scream coming from behind the door echoed through the hallway. Tristan tensed up and reached for the doorknob.

I Love You, Mona

Mona is confused and in disbelief. Is she that gullible to be manip- ulated that easy? Perhaps. How could she not know? How could she just fall into the trap like a fly in a spider's web? Now, the beast has full control of her body and she is encased within.

"Who are you?!?" she demanded at Claire. The latter looking heinous,her personality very far from the first time she appeared. She don't know her anymore.

"I am your mother. This is me, your Mom. Who else? The one you desired to meet, the one you wanted to be with. I am really who I am. I told you not to listen to those illusions..." Claire whispered as she slowly walk towards Mona, reaching out to her. "Tsk, tsk, tsk... Now, you're confused and it does not suit you, my dear..."

"No!" Mona screamed. "Don't touch me!! Don't ever come near me!" she warned, realizing that whenever she touches her, she can't seem to be herself. Sadly, she's just realizing it now that she had caused damage to her town. She backed away.

"What's the matter, dear? Don't you want to feel Momma's embrace?" Claire said smirking at her.

"No! Stay away!!" she yelled, not wanting to look at her anymore.

"Come on, Sweetie. Mom's here. Let me heal your pain. I'll just take a little more of your hatred and it will be over soon..." She coaxed Mona as she reached to her. Mona pushed her away.

"Stay away I said!! I know who you are! From this moment on, you will not control me. I am going to claim back my body and make everything right! You are not my mother and stop using her image! My mother will never ever do vile things like what you just made me do!" Mona snapped at Claire.

"How dare you! I am your Mother and you just pushed me away! How could I ever give birth to an ungrateful child! " Claire said angrily.

"If you are my mother, then give me a proof! Tell me about the day I was born. Tell me all about it! " Mona demanded, looking directly at Claire's eyes.

"I gave birth to you in a beautiful summer day. As if the universe has conspired to make it a brilliant and one of a kind day because it was the day you came to the world." Claire paused for a while before answering her confidently. Mona was startled.

"You were such a tiny bundle of joy and an outrageous one. I remember your cry, so loud but for me it was the most beautiful sound. I loved you the moment you were conceived to the time I held you for the first time. And I still love you now." Claire said dramatically, tears brimming in her eyes. "Come to me. Let me hold you once more my dearest..."

Mona tried her hardest not to fall again to her sugar-coated stories. She knew very well when and how she was born.

"Lies! You are a liar! A deceitful monster hiding in my body and a blasphemous one for using my Mom's image! Show your true self!!!" Mona yelled fiercely. This time, she knew better. Claire was startled but not for long, she just smirked at her.

"I was not born in a bright and sunny day. I was born in the middle of the night when the blue blood moon was shining down on earth. You are a liar!! Show true form!!!"

The image let out a very loud scream like that of a crazy banshee. Claire started to spread out like dye on water, and was then infused with a bright purple light. Then, the nine-tailed beast came out of the warped purple light.

"I can't believe you found out my disguise too soon. I was thinking I could use it for long. Well, hello Mona..." The beast said in a very deep voice that echoes in the confined room they are in. Mona stepped back as the beast come near her.

"Don't move away from me Mona. Let me see something else in you..." it said smirking.

"No! I will not let you use the people I love against me. You will die here and now you see! I'll kill you!" Mona warned firmly. It laughed maniacally.

"Tell me, how will you do it? You don't have your wolf!" with a swing of its tail, a wall cleared out and an unconcious Thalia appeared, looking very weak and in difficulty. She was bound by a silver chain on her neck.

"Thalia!" Mona screamed as she ran to her wolf. But as she get nearer, a force pulled her back so strong she was thrown to the other side of the room. She gasped for air as she hit the solid wall.

"I want you to know that there is nothing that can stop me. I have your body, I have your weakling of a wolf, and now, I will have your soul!!" It said in gritted teeth, walking very slowly towards her.

"Accept your fate Mona! I was kept for a million years in a vessel that is transferred to one body to another. But the bodies I had been were too weak, no one can open the lid of my vessel. Until I was transferred to your body. I am grateful to you and to everyone who feed me with darkness. Your miseries and sufferings were food to me, making me stronger until I was able to remove the lid and take over your wolf. She did gave a terrible fight against me but I am a celestial beast. I have the powers of the Moon and Sun and no lowly wolf can overcome me. I am grateful to the Luna for giving you the best torture ever! The moment you gave up your hope, I gained my freedom!! And I will not let anyone contain me again! Not any gods nor wolves or you!!! I'll devour your soul right here and now!" It laughed then leaped to Mona. It lunged to her and she was laid flat on the floor, the beast on top of her.

"No! You will not win! You will not have me! I swear I will defeat you!"Mona answered fiercely as the beast was pinning her to the floor. Drools of purplish saliva wetting her face.

The beast turned to mist and dived into her mouth. Mona gagged and she felt a rush of cold smoke flowing to her throat and settling in her stomach. An erupting pain burst all over her body that feels like her bones were breaking all at the same time, her lungs ran out of air, her heart being wringed and her head throbbing with ache she had not known. She went out of breath and it hurts like crazy she wailed loudly.

Tristan twisted the knob open and he can heared a deep voice speaking. The tone so deep it seems it is not from this world. And he heard every-thing it said, his eyes widening with its every word and revelation. He snapped back to his senses when he heard Mona's wail. He flung the door open and she saw her writhing in unbearable pain crumpled on the floor. Purple fog swirling about her and she's screaming pain. He ran towards her but the fog released dark electric shocks and threw him out. He was dazed for a while but he can clearly hear Mona's wails. He went again only to suffer the same thing but he did not bulge. Amidst the electric shocks that ran to his body, he stayed still. Determined to reach Mona no matter what.

"Mo--na...Mo--na..." He called to her, though she can't hear him. He called her louder fighting off the pain. His outstretched hand is starting to turn purple, soon enough it will be fried but he don't care. He forced himself in until blood drips from his arm. Mona looked at his way and he knew she saw him or so he thought

"Hold on Mona...I'll save you..." with much difficulty he was able to utter this words.

But Mona is failing, losing her battle against the beast. It will totally conquer her and Tristan will not permit that. He forced himself to the relentless fog barrier, never minding that it is grinding his body. He just hoped that his body is still intact if ever he pass through.

"I'll save you Mona. Hold on. I'm coming...." and with a last heave he went through the barrier face first on the floor, his body shaking. He creep to Mona's side, take her in his arms as he look down at her wide open dazed eyes, gaping mouth, shallow breaths and disheveled hair.

"Mona, it's me... It's Tristan... Stay with me." He said worriedly, gently stroking her hair. Mona was looking at him or the ceiling. He don't know whether she can see or feel him. He just hugged her tightly, whispering encouragement to her ears.

"Fight it Mona. You are strong , you are pure. You cannot be corrupted. You are stronger than you think you are..." Tristan whispered this repeatedly to Mona's ears. Mona on the other hand continued to jerk as if possessed by an evil spirit. Tristan tightened his embrace, not letting her go. He wanted her to know that she's not alone in this battle, that she can rely on him. If only...

Mona jerked incredibly, letting out pained moans, her mouth gaped as she inhaled air and her eyes flew open revealing her mismatched irises. Suddenly she saw a blurry face and though blurry, she knew the face too well. Somehow it brought her comfort. Her ears are ringing but amidst it, she can hear him. Urging her to fight, that she is strong, that she is incredible and she can overpower it. It brought her a warm feeling, relieving her of pain but not for long. She's drifting in and out and whenever she's back, she can see and hear him. This can't be a dream. He must be real. She called his name hoarsely and he responded avidly, smiling down at her. Somehow, her visions is clearing and she can see his face. Something warm dropped on her face and it gave her hope like rain in a desert.

"Tristan....are you real? Are you??" her voice rather hoarse and tired. She reached for his face, he immediately grabbed her hand and placed it on his cheek. He feels so warm and real and his smile is so bright. Now she's sure that Tristan is real.

"It's me. It is really me. I came to get you. We will go home now..." Tristan said, his voice hopeful and his face happy.

She smiled back to him. Tristan knew Mona is back. She defeated the beast, he knew she will. She helped her to sit down, gently and carefully. Her limbs are still like vegetables parched under the sun. He let her lean on him and watch out as she steadies her breathing.

"You're fine. You did great. I know you will defeat it. Thank you for coming back to me..." Tristan is overjoyed as Mona came back to her own conciousness. He leaned his forehead on hers and utter a silent grateful prayer to the Moon Goddess or whoever God was there that brought her back before he planted her a soft warm kiss on the lips.

Tristan kissed her and Mona knew that she is the happiest. They locked eyes and happiness is swimming on it together with an emotion she truly know the name of. As he breathes her in, she heard the one thing that she knew she had been yearning for all of her life, and it's finally here. Her eyes did not hold back tears of joy as Tristan pronounced it with sincere eyes showing the promise of tomorrow and the beauty that comes with it.

"I love you, Mona..."

The Last Descendant of the Sky

She looked at him with eyes that knows the truth and he smiled at her with sincerity. Mona knows that her world has started to turn towards the light, with Tristan beside her, giving her strength and love, she will make it.

"It has always been you and I am a fool not to know. The moment I saw you in the camp ten years ago, I know I was in trouble but I shrugged it off knowing that maybe I was just another curious fellow because you were different. But I was wrong. I never forgot about you. That night I failed to save you from the rogues always haunts me in my deepest sleep and I won't be able to forgive myself if you died that night..." Tristan said softy, almost whispering, his voice passionate.

"You live in my heart starting that night, and there you stayed until now. I was swayed all through these years because I am a faithful believer of the mate bond. Although deep inside, I wished that it's you - whom the Moon Goddess has made for me. Now it all makes sense. You may not be my mate but we are fated. Before, then and now. Because fate is not the work of any goddess, fate is a choice. And I choose you to be my fated one. And in a thousand lifetimes, it's you whom I will choose and if this life is not for us, I'll wait for you. I'll find you. Over and over again..." Tristan continued, letting his emotions flow like a river in a parched land, Mona drinking it all in. It feels so warm and joyful, this moment when Tristan recognizes his true feelings for her. So, this is how it feels to be loved back by the person who means a lot to you. Definitely, Mona can't have enough of it.

The beast has stopped moving. As if drained with energy or in zen mode, the spectators don't know what is going on its mind. Meanwhile, Tristan's body seems to be asleep too, near the beast's foreleg.

"Get my son out there!" William commanded. Few warriors immediately nodded and was about to collect Tristan.

"No, leave him be!" a forceful deep voice stopped the warriors on their way.

"He penetrated the beast's heart. Removing him will distract the connection. And if he lost it, we will lose this battle too." the Great Elder spoke behind William hoarsely, two younger pack members assists him. Willian recognizes them as Finn and Jake, the great great grand children of the Great Elder, who are both in their late adolescence. The High Elder is a very old man with a very long frizzy white beard that runs to his chest, just like those of common wizards in films; sagging wrinkly skin, ill-fitted in his thin frame, it seems to be not his skin at all, and his blue eyes now white from cataract.

"Let their souls speak. It is the only way to communicate to her because spoken words has no meaning for her now. We need words that can transcend through what the mind can comprehend , one that reaches the soul and the very core of the heart. Only the Young Master can do that. Because he is the yang to her yin. That is what they are. Connected since birth, complementing each other, and fated through time..." the Great Elder spoke amidst heavy breathing. In his age that is almost two centuries, little movements and even speaking tires him. Nonetheless, he managed to explain the situation they have.

"What should we do then Elder?" William asked the Elder, he seems to have lost his thinking faculties.

"We wait..." the Great elder said and nudged his great grandsons to assist him to a seat. His little venture did tire him.

"Let's go home, Mona. I still have to marry you. Let's begin our together now..." Tristan said smiling as he kisses her forehead. Mona nodded, smiling back at him. He took her hand to his and they opened the door so to leave the room.

Suddenly ,the beast stood up and growled loudly. Then, it grunted and yelped as if being attacked by an unknown force. Something is wrong with the beast. The warriors around stand on guard.

"What is happening now?" William asked worriedly.

"This is the final battle. A battle within. Let' s hope that she wins..." The Great Elder said, brooding.

Tristan and Mona were about to leave the room, hand in hand, when something pulled Mona back. She was thrown back to the room, flat on her back. She gasps for air suddenly feeling submerged in water. Tristan was about to go after her when he was pushed out of the room. He went to the door but it was locked. He was frantic, wanting to open the door to the point of wrecking it. But the door, though it looks old and has been eaten by termites, did not budge an inch. It did not even gave a care. Inside, the beast is back, giving Mona her finest torture yet.

"You will not claim anything from me! I am the owner of my body and you are an intruder! Harm me and I will destroy you for good!!" Mona yelled to the beast as it slap her face back and forth, blood starts to run down from her nose. But Mona has a newfound determination and strength, and she's sure, this beast will never beat her again. Without delay, she shifted to her wolf form, her body lighter and stronger, her mind more focused and determined to defeat the foe.

"It's good to be back!" Thalia echoed in her mind.

"Thanks Thalia! Now let's beat this beast together!!" Mona replied energetically to Thalia. The latter nod her head.

"Yes, let's beat her for good and let's go back to Tristan!" Thalia responded firmly, smirking. She's teasing her already.

Mona smiled, "To Tristan and to all the people who believes in me..."

A duel between the celestial beast and the moon wolf ensued. Tristan just heard growling, snarling and yelping from behind the door. Also thuds as a body hits the wall, Tristan has no idea whom. Then a strong breeze is pulling him away from the door. He tried to hold on the knob but it went with him. He was being sucked again to the void. And down, down , down he goes.

He gasps for air as he opened his eyes. He's back on his body and the first thing he saw was the beast in a crazed state. Tristan knew exactly what is happening, the fight between good and evil is happening right inside the deepest core of the beast. He moved away to avoid being stomped by the beast's giant legs. He's praying right now. To the Moon Goddess and all the Gods, that they may help Mona to defeat it. That's the only thing he can help her now aside from the constant shouting of encouragement from him.

Long time ago, after the Tale of the Moon was written by the very first elders. Another tale was written. It was the Tale of the Moon Wolf - the Descendants of the Sky.

It was true that the son of the Sun God and Moon Goddess who was known as the Sky God, fell in love with a maiden - a Moon Maiden - the first bloodline of the first werewolves. Because of that incident, when the Sky God choose the maiden over his dominion and status, it angered the Sun God which made him disown his one and only child and stripped him with all his titles and powers. Down to the Earth he was banished. The Moon Goddess wept day and night, pleading the Sun God to take back her son but he was rather stoic and proud. He did not heared her pleas.

Now, the Sky God also known as the Celestial Child, became a plain human being and married the maiden he loved . However, because of the Sun God's bitter distaste to the werewolves, he planted the Celestial Beast inside his son's body before stripping him with power, as a promise to destroy the werewolf race as he believed that they stole the Moon Goddess' and the Sky God's affection for him. It couldn't be denied that the Sun God was a jealous and possessive being, the reason he do what he did. Unknowingly, the Sky God became the vessel of the beast.

The first werewolves were known as the Moon Wolves, ruling all over the werewolves' race. There was no pack clans before and everything was nothing but harmonious. Later, being feed with greed and the love for power and dominion, a lot of werewolves aimed to have their own pack, separate from the Great Moon Pack. A mutiny rose between the strongest of the pack and the battle between the Alpha of Alphas happened. The Moon Goddess warned them that their kind will vanish if they continue fighting with each other. So, as a truce, the Moon Goddess divided the werewolf race into packs and appointed the strongest and wisest among them to lead each respective pack, as well as given them territories to man. Although retaining the Great Moon Pack as the Alpha of Packs for they are also the keeper of the Moon Stone. All other packs agreed and from then on, peace was restored to the packs.

Until the Celestial child came to Earth and married the Moon Maiden. She was the daughter of the Alpha of the Great Moon Pack - The Alpha Pack among the Packs. All Great Moon Pack members are known to have very light colored hair, silver or platinum blonde and their wolves were gigantic snow white wolves. And she was the gem of their pack. Soon, she gave birth to a child, a beautiful girl. But soon, when the child was nearing her 12th birthday, the beast escaped from her and killed her parents. But the celestial beast did not stayed long because it was still not in the perfect shape, its has a single tail then, which only means lesser power. It will gain another tail after a hundred years until it will complete its nine-tails over the years. Upon completing its nine-tails, it is said to be formidable and indestructible. Because it was still weak, the Great Moon Alpha mnaged to seal the beast again to her grand daughter's body. Soon, she grew up into a lovely woman and married a fine young lad. And the Celestial line continued.

After a hundred years, a man who was a direct descendant of the celestial child was overpowered by the celestial beast, once again it broke the seal and went amok. Causing havoc and chaos to the pack and it was successful. It wiped the Great Moon Pack for good. That is when the Moon Goddess came down to Earth to gave her aid. And it was defeated though not for good. Because it is a Celestial Beast and it's essence will continue to live as long as the Celestial bloodline is alive. It will transfer from one body to the next, so long as that body has the power and blood of the celestial child. They are what they call as the descendants of the sky. They became the outcast of the pack, ridiculed and feared for they are cursed. They can easily be identified by having a white moon hair, mismatched eye color, signifying the essence of the moon and the sun and their extraordinary strength. But they happen just once in a hundred years' generation of the celestial bloodline. Some descendants were born normally with the hair color same as their parents and the beast undisturbed within them until it was transfered to a more worthy body. That it why the truth about the descendants turned to memories and memories turned to tales.

It growled for one last time then the beast was covered with a purple fog and a bright ball of light. It dashed to the skies and came shooting down to Mona who was in her wolf form. Absorbing all of the celestial beast and sealing it within. Suddenly all turned silent, not even a single breath was heard. Mona shifted back to her body, feeling very weak. Tristan went to her in time to catch her. He embraced her tightly and covered her naked body with a table cloth laying around the ground zero. She returned his embrace, happy and grateful for his help.

"I am happy that you're back." Tristan whispered thankfully.

"Yes. I came back for you..." she looked up at him smiling with loving eyes. Tears falling one by one.

"Thank you mylove. I want to say it again, I love you and no one else will come before you. I love you so much, promise me you'll stay..." Tristan speaks up in her face, determined and passionate. Mona touched his face lovingly, smiling sweetly back at him.

"I promise to ----" Mona did not finished her words, blood rushed from her mouth, her face in extreme agony, her eyes was first in shock then sorrowful..." Tristan widened his gaze and saw a glowing pinkish arrow has struck Mona's back, hitting straight to her heart. He looked around and saw the culprit.

"Never again will the beast trample on our kind! She must be killed to stop the curse! I shot the arrow that ends it! Luna, I killed her for you!!! I killed the last descendant of the Sky!!!" yelled by a manic Bruce, whose body was also battered and bathing in his own blood. The warriors grappled him to the ground, he never stopped shouting it, repeating over and over again until one silenced him. He lay there with a couple of warriors around him, bleeding unconciously.

"Tris-tan...."Mona called as her knees gave away. Tristan crying over her, still in disbelief, touching her face. It is very painful but she knew it will be the last she'll see his beautiful face, the face she loved so much.

"No, No, Mona...stay with me.. Stay..." Tristan said frantically, he was too sad and his tears were like rain. He was sobbing. Why does it hurt like this? He leaned his ear to her lips as she breathe her last words.

"I ---I -- love -- you...." was her final words as she choked with blood and closed her heavy lids.

Up Where She Belongs

B eads of sweat come rushing down on Tristan's face, intermixed with his tears and saliva, sobbing and yelling for help. This can't be happening! He felt her neck for pulse but it has none. Not a single heartbeat. Moments later, medical attendants came in and gave her first aid. Futile as it is, they still tried reviving her but she's gone. Tristan gaped, unwilling to accept the fact that Mona is dead. His father held his shoulder for a long time as he cried like he never did before, right there embracing her lifeless body.

"She's gone, son..." William whispered. As a proof, he showed his left arm to him and broken silvery threads are falling off and are slowly dissipating into thin air. A sign that they are now free of the unbreakable bond, that the person whom they have sworn their protection has died. He saw it too, as the silvery threads shed off his arm.

"I failed. I failed to protect her... I am useless!" Tristan cried as he helplessly look at the shedding silver threads in his arm.

"Don't say that, you did your very best to bring her back. You saved her..." William assured him.

"Then I let her die..." Tristan added, now looking at her peaceful face. Never again will he see the warmth in her eyes and the sweetness in her smile. It made him feel terrible. He has plans for them after this chaos. He still wanted to make her feel how it is to be truly loved and cared for. Now his chance has gone with the wind.

Bill came in slowly and weakly to where Tristan is, assisted by Troy who was also battered, his face filled with bruises and sporting a black eye. Bill felt it when Mona was slayed and as she let go of her last breath. Something in him broke apart and he knew, it will be irreparable. Now he wished that he just died wheb the beast trampled him.

Troy himself felt terrible and a failure. He stands as Mona's guard, sworn to protect her with his life but he failed completely. Seeing his master died in his watch and he was not able to help much during her despair is not a very convincing quality of a Guardian. Now that Mona is gone, he is free too. The imprint will vanish as soon as the master shut her eyes for good. Troy can't help but pity and blame himself for his lack of attention and foresight.

The night breeze sings of lament.

"She is indeed the last descendant of the Sky. And her death is also the death of the celestial beast." The Great Elder spoke behind them, in his very hoarse throaty voice.

"Don't despair, Son. For it is written. She was born under the blue blood moon, she died under a great Oak Moon which symbolizes the completion of purpose and the fulfillment of a promise..." he said mystically as he looks up in the bright moon. They look at it too, mesmerized with its beauty and mystery.

It suddenly felt cold, the night air turned chilly and a little foggy. They saw it too, two bright lights from the moon were falling freely to them, it slowed down when it was near the ground so it won't explode from the impact. It's like two balloons fleeting on the ground, very light and warm and surreal. They felt a rush of warm and refreshing energy rushing through their body. The two bright lights wear off its blinding lights and it revealed two mystical people. The people whom they only have acquaintance with in the books. The Sun God, in his dashing, powerful and striking features. Every inch of him speaks dominance and greatness. While the other one is a beautiful woman that emits a lovely and tranquil effect to anyone who sees her. She is the stark contrast to the man beside her. When he was all power and rage, she is tranquility and serenity. The celestial couple. The Sun God and Moon Goddess in flesh and bones right in front of their very eyes. Everyone went down on their knees and bowed low. Troy, though his head was bent knows he had seen the lady before, only he can't remember where and how.

"You did great, child." The Moon Goddess spoke in her ethereal voice, lifting all their weariness.

Troy immediately turn his head to her.

" It was not a battle lost. This is exactly where everything is supposed to be..." she continued.

"It has been the plan all along." The Sun God speaks in his high and mighty tone.

"Do not despair, for all of you were pieces of the game. And in a game, not every one wins. But in this, you all win as you are freed with the threat of the Celestial Beast." The Sun God continued.

An riotious, manic laugh broke the silence from the pack.

"See? Even the Gods favor the deed I made!" Bruce spoke up, staggering as he move closely to the Gods. He stopped in front of them and knelt low, kissing their feet.

"I am your lowly servant, my King and Queen of Heavens. I am honored to complete the deed..." Bruce said sneering.

Tristan and Troy on the other hand are disgusted with Bruce. If only he could smack him one more time, it would feel really good then. Troy is angry especially now he recalled where she's seen the lady goddess before.

"So this was the purpose of saving her ten years ago! Why not let her die when she fell on the Moon River? I know it was you! The Healer in Oakwood Grove, are you not? It was you who pulled out us out in the water. Why prolong her sufferings when you could just let us drown then and there?!" Troy said firmly, he said as tears of hate glints in his eyes. The Great Elder let out a gasp of terror hearing Troy's accusing tone to the Goddess.

"You are correct. That was me, my human form who dwell in Oakwood Grove, Karen Sage. She and I are one. But I did what has to be done. It was not yet the right time for her to be taken and so you too." she said calmly.

"So you mean, you let her live more years to experience all these world's cruelties, miseries and sufferings brought by her own pack!? What for?!" Troy yelled, very enraged. Bill stopped him, still he is talking to the Gods, he must show respect. But Troy is unstoppable, eaten by his hate and disappointment. The Sun God himself frowned with his rough behavior.

"For second chances, my dear child. I believe in second chances. I was hoping that all will change after the incident. That everyone will learn to accept the girl who survived the Moon River. As you all know, a fall in the Moon River is as good as death for you will fall directly to the realms of the dead. No one comes back once you plunge into it, no one survives. But here you are, the two of you." She smiled calmly at Troy, stepping towards him.

"I saved the two of you because I believe in the goodness of your race. But I was wrong..." Her heavenly face suddenly fills with disappointment. "The pack still cast her aside. Ridiculed, judged and humiliated her to the core. But it did not destroy her though, you know why? Because she has you. My decision to pull you out of the water was correct for you saved her, supported her all through those trying, miserable years. You did your purpose excellently, I cannot ask for more. That is why I truly understand your distress right now. But I assure you, no one will be better with the job than you... " She smiled and tapped Troy's arm. He instantly felt a feeling of warmth not from this world, washing his worries and distress away. Then she looked at Bruce, her sweet innocent face suddenly turned scary and dreadful.

"This man will still be punished severely for taking a life which he has no right of. Only us, the Gods can take back what we give to you and no one else." With a snap, Bruce seems to be coming out of breath, gasping air like a fish out of the water and a white fog was lifting out of his body. Is it supposed to be his soul? But one thing is real, the Moon Goddess is taking Bruce's life away from him. The last thing of Bruce is a lifeless body lying on the ground, his face purple and petrified.

"I wish I should have not done it but I have to. Because we Gods, are just and fair. He took one, I let him pay for it. Still, I want to thank you for restoring my faith in your kind, Bill. This is the second chance that I was saying. And William, thank you for leading your pack well. Claire sends her regards to both of you..."

"Her untimely death is not what I intended, but it happened somehow. I will take her with me. Up to the sky where she belongs. There she will never feel sadness, oppression, and misery. She will be free... " The Sun God approached Tristan who was holding her body. He held it tighter and buried his head on her neck. William tapped his shoulder to let go.

"Your love is pure and true. But what is it when the one you intend to offer it with was gone?" The Sun God said straigthly as he held his powerful arms, taking Mona away from him.

"Forgive my husband. He is rather straightforward and harsh but I swear, he is a kind and temperate man. I see your pain Tristan. And I see your love that is so pure and true. One day, you'll find each other again and when you do, believe that I, the Moon Goddess blessed your fate." she said dignified. She gave her attention to the crowd, who were eager and waiting for her every word, drinking her presence like an intoxicating wine.

"The Moon Stone has very little power now. It was almost exhausted during the feat with the celestial beast. You all know what will happen if it's gone. You will become savages and I dont want it to happen again. You as my beloved species. So accept this gift." The Moon Goddess went near to Mona's body, now carried by the Sun God. The arrow that was struck in her was slowly removed. She placed her hands in front of Mona's chest and a bright ball of white light came from it.

"This is the purest of all hearts known to your kind. This is Mona's heart. Her final gift to your kind. She was an outcast but she has a gentle and pure heart to forgive you all, amidst all you did to her. Place this with the Moon Stone and it will be restored back to what it was. If ever you are in the brink of evil, remember Mona and her forgiving, pure heart..." She handed the glowing white ball of light to the Great Elder who bowed low as he received the gift, muttering gratitude to the Goddess.

"May you live in harmony and peace with each other. And let there be no other Mona who will be outcasted from any pack... " The Moon Goddess' farewell words.

"But before we go, let my husband, the Sun God restore your town. It was his beast that did this. So it is his responsibility to restore order from the chaos he planted. " She smirked to her husband, the latter flustered stood in attention. With a snap of his fingers, everything came back to normal. The buildings, the landscape and all are returning one by one to its proper places and previous appearance.

"This is farewell then. I bless you all with bliss and harmony." With that, they turned into two ball of lights again and spurted to the skies, taking with them Mona's body.

Tristan just gazed for a long time to the one gift that she left for them, the Great Elder holding it firmly and protectively as a treasure. After all she'd been through, she still left them a gift for their redemption. Her heart. The purest of all.

To the Moon and Back

" **M**aybe the wolf is in love with the moon, And each month it sings for a love That it will never reach... " - Anonymous

Every month he howls singing his song of love to her maiden up above. And as the moon changes, he barely noticed that it has been years since she's gone. Ten solid years of despair and emptiness. She died but his love for her did not. It still burns brightly giving him strength in facing day after day.

Tristan Jones is now the Alpha of the Black Moon Pack and he is still yearning for his irreplaceable Luna. Ten years and it was still her and no one else comes close.

Miranda Jones, the former Luna of the pack, after surviving the ordeal with the celestial beast was banished as her punishment for torturing Mona, thus awaking the beast within her. The Grand Alpha himself gave the sentence, but it went through a rigid deliberation process with the other Alphas. Indeed, she was the root of the chaos and it was just right to banish her from the pack. Not long, they heard that Miranda, overwhelmed by her banishment, jumped off to the Moon River. Since then, no one has heard of her.

Three years after the incident, Tristan was crowned the new Alpha of the Black Moon Pack, right on his twenty-fifth birthday. He could have been happier if only his Luna was there to pin him the badge of responsibility. He appointed Troy Brooks as his beta, Henry Mason as the gamma. Since then, their bond have become stronger as that of brothers. Troy married Joyce Wilson and he was the godfather of their first born, whom they named Tiana (in honor of him, Tristan and Mona.) Whereas, Henry and Leizel are married for eight years and are now expecting their second child. And all of them were free of the remnants of the broken bond, and so their lives were nothing but peaceful.

Through those years, so many women had tried to please him. As an Alpha and to continue their line, it was his reponsibility though try hard as he may, his heart has a mind of its own. It did not want to open up and love again.

The Grand Elder place Mona's heart rightafter the chaos, thus restoring the Moon Stone, serving its purpose of helping their kind to retain their sanity and not turn to monsters and savages. Since then, everyone has regarded Mona higher than anyone else. She has become the epitome of goodwill and hope to their entire race.

It has been ten years of peace and harmony among the packs. Ten years and amidst his little achievements, there is an emptiness in him that no one else can fill.

He was on their veranda again, his usual place, leaning on the railing and talking to the moon, his father appeared behind him.

"Lost in thoughts?" William said, now a little bent with age. Bill Mayfield died five years ago, the injury he got from the beast's attacks did not totally healed plus his grief of losing yet another important part of his life made him sickly. He died on a full moon and he was buried next to his beloved wife. He left Troy his estate as he treated the man as his own since Mona had died, and the latter, took care of him as he was battling with the illness which at last, consumed him.

Tristan simply nodded. He loves solitude more than ever. He appreciates the time he is not surrounded by his overwhelming paperworks in the office and the noisy packhouse. He is more himself here in this veranda, the moon shining down on him. His father clears his throat.

"It is really hard to forget. You know, Son. When I was young, I loved a wonderful woman, more than I loved your Mom. We made plans for our future together but as you see, fate did not allow it. Since then, no matter who I meet, or who I lay in bed with, it was always her. In my mind, and in my heart. Yes, I did love another woman, but she remained my constant. Do you get me? You are not getting any younger Tristan. I know Troy and Henry had been talking you with this but let me talk to you about it again...." His father spoke sincerely and totally fatherly. Yet, Tristan knows where this talk is heading. He's been into this a million times before and the idea for him is nothing but vague.

"You are an Alpha and you have a responsibility to the pack. You need an heir. It's time to let Mona go..." he said softly. He looked at his father intently, what he said irritates him. William sensed his irritation, still he added.

"You have to face the reality, son. You are alive and don't waste your youth over a dead girl. I'm sorry. I am not asking you to forget her though..."

"And what do you mean by that?!" Tristan retorted, his father's remarks wounding him.

"You can still love her in silence. In the solitude of the night and think of her as you sing your songs to the moon. As I said a million times before not all love story ends happily. Some ends tragicly like yours and Mona's. It ended even before you two had started. Believe me, I am sad with it too. You know how I liked her for you, not because she was her mother's daughter but because she was gentle and nice and kind. I can't see a better match for you but her."

William took a deep breath before he continued. "But all love is eternal especially if its true. When you find your one great love it never fades. It will never die. Tangible or intangible, it remains as a heart-warming memory and a blissful strength that will keep us moving towards the light." William said full of wisdom.

"You cannot force yourself to love anew, but remember your responsibility to our bloodline. The Jones has been here for centuries and it will not stop in your watch..." He said it in a very fatherly tone but with hints of authority. The Alpha in him is still in full instinct. He left him alone to ponder on this thought. He sighed deeply.

"Alpha? Alpha! Are you listening?" Troy nudged him, they are in his office and yes, he is spacing out. He suddenly went back to his senses as if a bolt of electricity stun him for a moment.

"What were you saying, Troy?" he said, placing his hand on his chin, stroking his non-exsistent beard. Troy rolled his eyes as he repeats his report.

"A group of human beings has been spotted near our northern territory, just past the Northern woods. It seems that the human government has made the majestic falls a tourist attraction, that's why humans are flocking there. Also, they had started building cabins near the falls as camp for tourists. "

"I don't see problems with that. Humans are harmless and they dont have an inkling that the nearest town from the falls is filled with werewolves." he said uninterestingly. "They are not a threat to us."

"But Alpha, remember that we have a camp up in the Northern Woods that serves as a training ground for our pups! What if someone stalked too near our bounds and sees us, shifting from human to our wolf form? It will be bad news."

"For humans, werewolves are unreal and were just myths. If someone will see us, no one will believe them." He said spinning in his swivel chair like a foolish child.

"We should not overlook them just because they are harmless, weak human beings. You see, they can harm us too; they have weapons and gadgets--" Troy said firmly but was cut midsentence.

"And we are enjoying them too. How many of our pups have become addicted to those mobile games and social media stuffs instead of training? That must be addressed first." He said turning back to Troy who looks exasperated.

"Alright. Alright. I'll check it out myself. If it will truly endanger our security, I'll have more border guards to scare any human that will go astray. Better? " He said to Troy, trying not to laugh in his sour facial expression. "Besides, I'll be needing extra stretching. Cover up for me!" with that he shifted to his wolf form and dashed out of the door, leaving a dumbstruck Troy behind.

He loves this. The feeling of the wind on his fur. The strength of his legs as he leaps and runs. The scent of the woods. He went to the Northern Camp, and locate his extra clothes. Shifting sometimes is a head ache. Once you go back to your human form, you'll be as naked as a baby. And in this era, going out to places naked will get you arrested. Reason why they hid clothes on selected locations in case of emergency just like now. He dressed up.

He leisurely walked to where the Majestic falls is. Very silently, not a twig or a dried leaf has snapped while he walk by. At last, he can hear the sound of the rushing waterfalls yet he smells something delicious and so, so familiar it made his heart race.

He remembers stalking Mona when they were youngsters in the camp, twenty or more years ago. He silently followed her to the falls and watched her happily as she made sketches in her sketch book. She looks content and happy in where she was and that was the first time he heard his heart beats louder than before. As he came near the spot, the smell is getting stronger too like honeysuckle and peonies and only one person owns this particular scent.

"One day you'll meet again, and once you do, believe that I, the Moon Goddess has made it possible and blessed your fate..."

A distant memory whispers back these words to him and he can't stop but be hopeful. Right on the very spot where young Mona once occupied, concentrating and drawing in her sketch book, was a woman. A woman whom he knew too well. He can't believe it yet the goddess' words keep flowing in his mind, repeating over and over again like a melodious song.

A woman was there, busily painting in her canvass. She's wearing a mustard sweatshirt and faded jeans topped with a paint-blotched apron . She's holding a palette on her left hand and a brush on her right, gently doing some brush strokes in her already done canvass. Her auburn hair is tied in a messy bun, loose hair being swept by the gentle wind, same as her plum-colored feather earrings. The outline of her face is so familiar yet different. But he knew in his heart who she is.

The girl, realizing his presence stopped working and looked at him. And one look is enough to stop the world from spinning. Nothing else matters but them.

She looks at him as if she'd known him forever and his eyes looks at her like it was she he had been waiting his whole life. She even stopped breathing, the brush and palette in her hands fell without her noticing. No one speaks a word, afraid it might ruin the magic.

How could he forget that face who always occupied his dreams and mostly his waking hours? That hazel eyes intoxicating him and her lips that could quench his thirst? He moves one step at a time and very slowly as if a slowmo until he's just inches away from her.

"Is this really you??" he whispered, his breath shaking.

"Yes..." she slowly replied, looking at his face, as if remembering a very lost and distant memory.

"For real??" he cupped her soft cheeks in his hands. It felt warm and real so her must not be dreaming.

She nods. "Now I remember, where I saw you. Not in my dreams. Not in my visions but in my heart. You were there in my heart, keeping me awake at night. You were the one who sings for me under the moon. It reached me. It reached me and made me come back for you... " she said her tone filled with longing and happiness she can't deny.

"Mona... " he whispered as a tear glided his face "Yes, Tristan my love. It's me... " she reached for his lips and kissed it with all the love she have.

"But how??" Tristan asked when the kiss ended.

"It's her." He pointed to the canvass and he saw the portrait of the Moon Goddess, sitting in her heavenly throne petting a marvelous snow-white wolf and the celestial beast at the same time. He hugged her tightly, and silently uttered a prayer of thanks to the Moon Goddess who granted his yearnings.

"I am back and no longer one of you. I am now a human... " she said silently. Now she remembers how the goddess sent her back. Apparently she hears his songs to the moon and it breaks her heart. He removed her wolf in her and gave her a mortal human body in exchange. Until then, she will not remember anything about her and her past life. For a long time she feels so lost and desolate, not until she went on a vacation in this part of the earth that somehow made her heart at peace. As if she is connected to this place, here she stayed for a year now, painting thoughts and fragments of memories she is not sure whom. Until today that everything is revealed. And when they meet, truly their hearts have known.

"All I know is I love you. More than ever, more than anything... " She whispered as her tears fall.

"And I love you too, to the moon and back... " he replied and kissed her forehead, seeing brighter days ahead of them.

**** The End****